The Secondhand Earl

SECOND TIME BRIDES, BOOK 2

BY
SKY PURINGTON

Text by Sky Purington
Cover by Dar Albert

Dragonblade Publishing, Inc. is an imprint of Kathryn Le Veque Novels, Inc.
P.O. Box 23
Moreno Valley, CA 92556
ceo@dragonbladepublishing.com

Produced in the United States of America

First Edition September 2023
Trade Paperback Edition

ARE YOU SIGNED UP FOR DRAGONBLADE'S BLOG?

You'll get the latest news and information on exclusive giveaways, exclusive excerpts, coming releases, sales, free books, cover reveals and more.

Check out our complete list of authors, too!

No spam, no junk. That's a promise!

Sign Up Here

www.dragonbladepublishing.com

Dearest Reader;

Thank you for your support of a small press. At Dragonblade Publishing, we strive to bring you the highest quality Historical Romance from some of the best authors in the business. Without your support, there is no 'us', so we sincerely hope you adore these stories and find some new favorite authors along the way.

Happy Reading!

CEO, Dragonblade Publishing

Additional Dragonblade books by Author Sky Purington

Second Time Brides Series
Never Second Guess a Lord (Book 1)
The Secondhand Earl (Book 2)

Highlander's Pact Series
Scoundrel's Vengeance (Book 1)
Scoundrel's Fortune (Book 2)
Scoundrel's Redemption (Book 3)

The Lyon's Den Series
To Tame the Lyon

Pirates of Britannia Series
The Seafaring Rogue
The Sea Hellion

What happens when unexpected love is met with a damning secret?

Lady Grace Howard and her ailing son have no choice but to move in with her sister Maude and her husband. Although welcome, she is too prideful to remain with them overly long. So when she crosses paths with a cynical war-wounded earl who needs her dowry but loathes the idea of falling in love again as much as she, Grace agrees to a marriage of convenience. Little does she know there is more to the bargain. Something she would not have liked one bit.

While Charles, Lord of Newcastle, needs Grace's dowry, the business her brother-by-marriage brings to his port is the driving force behind marrying her. It's something she must not know about, lest her pride land her in the arms of the wrong suitor. Despite preferring honesty, he agrees without understanding how much hiding the truth might cost him. But then, he could not anticipate how fond of each other they would become. How much they would help heal one another's hearts. Moreover, he could have never foreseen passion—let alone love—igniting between them. Now his secret will likely become a damning truth.

Will Charles and Grace be able to weather the storm when it comes? Or is their marriage doomed to be as superficial as initially intended?

Chapter One

Cheshire, England
24 August 1817

LADY GRACE HOWARD stared out her bedroom window at the sweeping countryside, blinked back tears, and tried to forget how she had felt the first time she stood there. The love she'd had for the man she just married. How excited she had been for their future together.

Over a year had passed since she lost her husband, William, and while beyond the stark pain that once made it impossible to get out of bed, she still suffered. Only now, it was in silence. A ceaseless melancholy hidden away so she might show her son, Alexander, the strength he needed to see.

"The carriage is ready, my lady." Her maid and dearest friend, Catlin, rested a hand on her shoulder. "It is time to say goodbye."

Too emotional to speak, she managed a weak nod.

"Alexander needs to see you strong now more than ever, my lady." Sympathy mixed with strength in Catlin's warm brown eyes. "As do I, if I were to be honest. I do so worry about you."

"I know," she whispered and cleared her throat. "And strength you shall see." Taking a few more moments, she rested her hand over Catlin's on her shoulder. "To that end, I insist you cease calling me 'my lady' when we are alone. It feels far too formal."

Welsh-born, Catlin had been with Grace since she married her late husband. He had hired her not because she was qualified but out of the kindness of his heart. Since then, Grace had coached her into becoming a suitable lady's maid, and their relationship had blossomed into a deep friendship akin to that of a mother and daughter.

"Be that as it may, I must get in the practice of addressing you correctly." Catlin gave her a pointed look. "We have enjoyed an unusual relationship considering my position. Now, as we reenter proper society, it is best I utilize all you taught me when I first came under your employ."

"I suppose you are right." She sighed. "Best you try to master it straight away, though, so we can return to normal in private."

The corner of Catlin's mouth curled up. "I will do my very best, my lady."

"I hope so."

Catlin's delicate snow-white brows swept up. Fine lines fanned from the corners of her eyes when her smile grew. "Do you doubt me? Surely not." She squeezed Grace's hand. "Whatever lies ahead, however proper I might seem, I am always me on the inside, dear friend. Always here for you no matter what."

"And I could not be more thankful." She gazed out the window one last time and nodded. "Truly thankful for both you and Hew."

Hired to tutor Alexander when she could no longer afford to keep him in boarding school, Hew was Catlin's cousin. While a rather strict sort, he came at a fair price, and he and her son got along well. Like Catlin, he was willing to travel with her and continue with Alexander's studies for as long as Grace could afford him.

"I suppose it is time," she finally said, squaring her shoulders. "Have we everything we need for Alexander?"

By *need*, she meant coffee and various helpful elixirs for when his hay fever flared up. Anything to help him breathe better if he suffered one of his attacks. They had moved from London years ago to escape the coal dust, finding the countryside more beneficial. Now they were en route to Scotland and a new variety of dust and dander that could cause just as much trouble because he was unused to it.

"We do have everything young Alexander needs, my lady." Catlin held out her elbow. "Shall we?"

"And here I thought you were determined to be proper."

"Oh, I will be." Catlin nodded once as if a soldier readying herself to go to battle. "Once we are on our way."

Grace breathed a sigh of relief and linked her arm with Catlin's. "Thank goodness."

The walk downstairs was difficult. How could it not be when she had loved every little nook of her home? When every spot seemed to possess a cherished memory? Her throat tightened, and her shoulders grew heavy. Determined to face an uncertain future, she blinked back tears and kept putting one foot in front of the other. Her butler, who had vowed to open the door one last time for her, did just that. If that were not touching enough, she found her servants lined up in the drive to bid her farewell. She had thought they had left already, but it seemed not.

Grateful for each and every one, wishing she could have afforded to keep them on, she managed a goodbye to all and climbed into the carriage. While tempted to gaze out the window at her house one last time, she set aside her sadness and focused on her son.

"How are you, darling?" She forced a smile. "Are you excited to see MacLauchlin Castle?"

"I am, Mother." He offered a proper nod. "It shall be quite something, I imagine."

While his deep green eyes had shone with excitement at the thought of journeying there before his father passed, his inner light appeared snuffed out now. Instead, he seemed a shell of his former self. His shock of pale blond hair might have been ruffled before, but now it was neatly, if not painfully, brushed back without nary a lock askew. He rarely smiled. Never laughed. He seemed another boy altogether. Kind as ever, but still much changed and it broke her heart. She missed the carefree, happy boy he used to be.

"I imagine it *will* be something." She kept a warm smile firmly in place and hoped her gaze reflected the excitement she tried to muster for him. "After all, MacLauchlin Castle is over five hundred years old with such an amazing history." Sure to round her eyes in awe, she reminded him just how special it was. "And to think your Uncle MacLauchlin's ancestors have always called it theirs."

"Indeed." A brief glimpse of sadness flickered in Alexander's eyes when he glanced out the window at their former home, fading into the distance. "I look forward to seeing it."

Did he truly? Because she got the sense he dreaded it. Perhaps related it to the visit they were supposed to have made before his father grew ill. *A grand adventure to a proper Scottish castle from another time*, as William had phrased it. He had been looking forward to bringing Alexander there.

So, she was determined to be equally passionate about it for their son.

She wanted him to find happiness again. Be the boy he once was. Hopefully, leaving their house and its endless reminders of the past would be a good first step. Or so she prayed, because they had no choice. William's estate was reverting back to his family, leaving her with little more than what she began with, the remains of a meager dowry which she would use to keep Hew and Catlin in her employ for as long as she could.

It would take more than half the day to get to MacLauchlin Castle, so everyone settled into their usual conversation, which was, in this case, Hew giving Alexander a history lesson as they traveled. A means to lend some anticipation to what lay ahead. About halfway, they stopped for a picnic lunch of buttered biscuits and cold tea, then continued on their journey.

"Oh, goodness," Catlin exclaimed when they started down a

narrow, winding drive lined with silver birches and towering pines later that day. "How enchanting and a tad mysterious, is it not?" She grinned at Alexander. "Like something out of one of those books you enjoy reading."

"It certainly is." Grace smiled at the old, twisted trees they passed to MacLauchlin Castle when it appeared in all its medieval glory. "And just look," she exclaimed. "It even has a drawbridge."

Was that a spark of interest in Alexander's eyes when he took in everything, or wishful thinking on her part? She could only hope the former. The inside of the castle was as intriguing as the outside, or so she had been told by her sister Maude who she could see flying down the front steps toward them, at their approach.

While she would never pick favorites when it came to her three sisters, she could admit Maude had always been the most entertaining. Where some might have thought her marrying a viscount would have curbed her unconventional, joyful ways, it had not, based on the way she greeted them. The moment the footman opened the door, she stuck her head into the carriage and offered them a wide smile.

"Welcome, dear family." Her lively, cinnamon-colored eyes were bright as ever, and her crop of brown curls were wild beneath her bonnet. She clasped her hands together in delight. "How splendid to see you all again." After nodding hello to Hew and Catlin, she offered Grace a tender, sympathetic look before holding out her hand to Alexander. Her smile grew especially merry. "Come, dear nephew. I cannot wait to show you around MacLauchlin Castle, but first, let us enjoy some sweets, yes?"

"That would be very nice, my lady."

"Goodness, no." Maude waved off the proper address and made things clear. "As you know, I insist you only ever call me Aunt Maude, Auntie Maude, or even Auntie Maude MacLauchlin. Do get creative if you wish." She winked and chuckled. "Within reason, of course. Yet still, any other form of aunt that makes you smile is sure to be quite lovely."

When Alexander glanced with uncertainty from Hew to Grace, she nodded. "I tend to agree, as she is your aunt."

Not just that, but Maude would eventually get her way no matter what.

"It is settled then." Maude helped Alexander out of the carriage where her husband Blake awaited them. He and her sister had visited Grace several times during her mourning period, and she had always found him kind. In fact, his demeanor had put her mind at ease about staying here until she could figure out what to do next.

"How are you, darling sister?" Maude linked arms with her, and they headed up the stairs behind Blake and Alexander. Her eyebrows knit. "You have said in your letters that things have grown easier with time, but still, I worry about you."

"I am well." Or so she was determined to claim. "No need to worry."

"Yet I will because that is what sisters do." Maude's gaze swept over her. "Not to mention you still wear black, even though you are beyond your mourning period."

"I feel it best." She gestured in Alexander's direction. "You understand."

"Do I?" The corners of Maude's mouth tugged down, and even though her tone remained compassionate, she was blunt as ever. "Would it not do him good to see you in something slightly more vibrant? Better put, dressed in something that is not a constant reminder of all you have lost?"

"I cannot say," she said softly, struggling to remain the calm, collected sister Maude knew when she felt anything but at the moment. Rather, she felt more unstable than she had when leaving her home. She teetered on the edge of fresh pain that had everything to do with what should have been. How she should have walked up these very steps for the first time with William.

"Oh, dear," Maude said just as softly before she stopped and looked at Grace with her heart in her eyes. "I *knew* you were putting on a brave face in your letters." She shook her head. "I knew you did not want me worrying about you."

She tried to respond but could not get a word in edgewise as her sister continued,

"Well, I *am* worried about you and intend to see you free from such melancholy." Maude brushed an escaped curl back from Grace's face like she used to when they were children. "I cannot tell you how glad I am that you have come to live with us." She cupped Grace's shoulders and nodded with reassurance. "We shall find joy in your life once more, dear sister. I promise you that."

Was such possible? It seemed hard to believe.

It also seemed a daunting statement, given what she knew of Maude.

"While I am thrilled you helped our sister, Prudence, find love again—" she shook her head—"I do not wish the same." She made things perfectly clear. "I have no intention of remarrying, let alone falling in love, so do not think to play matchmaker."

"I would *never*." Maude's eyes rounded. She pressed her hand to her heart. "Surely, you do not think that is why I invited you here? That I would ever press such a thing when I know you need time?"

"The thought had crossed my mind." Then, focusing on the clever way Maude liked to word things, she gave her sister a look. "And do not think that will change after *time* either."

"Goodness gracious, no," Maude agreed. Yet Grace swore she saw a glimpse of cunning in her sister's eyes before they continued up the stairs, and she redirected the conversation to a lighter topic. "Tell me everything I have missed since last we wrote. Do not leave out a thing."

So she did, and they spent an enjoyable evening together on her first night at MacLauchlin Castle. As glorious inside as it was outside, she was taken in by the spacious great hall and numerous old-world furnishings. Everything was eye-drawing, from the massive tapestries to medieval weaponry to the vast portraits staring down. With numerous hallways leading to what seemed an endless number of rooms, this was bound to be an exciting place for her and her son to live.

It was, too.

At least for Alexander, over the next month.

Hew and Catlin were made to feel welcome and received comfortable accommodations in the servants' quarters. Her son still had his daily lessons from Hew, but she asked that they be fewer while they adjusted to their temporary home. Besides, she wanted to spend time with Alexander and especially wanted him to interact and visit with his aunt and uncle, both of whom were quite taken with him.

"He is a lovely boy, Grace," Maude said one afternoon as the two of them worked on their latest embroideries in front of the fire. "You must be very proud."

"He is, and I am." She considered the faraway, somewhat sad, look in her sister's eyes and spoke to it. Tried to assure Maude that all would be well. "Soon enough, you will experience such pride for your own child. Just give it time."

"Of course." Maude rested her hand absently on her womb. "Just time…"

"Indeed." She placed her hand over Maude's and offered a comforting smile. "These things *do* take time, so be patient. You and Lord MacLauchlin will have a child. I am certain of it."

"Yet it has been quite a while and nothing." She sighed. "Too long when you and Prudence conceived so quickly."

"I might have, but Prudence did not in her last marriage," she reminded. "Every woman is different. You know that."

"I suppose so," Maude said softly. "Yet still, I cannot help but wonder…worry."

"And that is perfectly natural." Certain she was right because no one had more love to give than Maude, she shook her head. "But you need not worry because your time *will* come."

"I can only hope and pray." Not one to linger in melancholy long, a twinkle swiftly replaced sadness in her sister's eyes. "While I adore your vote of confidence, Grace, I cannot help but point out you sound a tad more like your old self right now." Her eyebrows whipped up. "Could it be your new home agrees with you?"

While Grace had written all three sisters often over the years, she had corresponded with Maude the most after William passed away, sharing things with her she held back from Prudence and Abby—Prudence because she was starting out in a bright new life and did not deserve anything bringing her down, and Abby because she struggled so much in her own marriage. Why add to her worries?

On top of all that, Maude was just Maude. Her dear, sweet, upbeat, older sister who supported her no matter what. Someone with whom she could confide everything since the very beginning. That is until now when she realized just how poignant Maude's pain was that she had yet to conceive.

"My new home *does* agree with me." Careful not to look unsettled or ungrateful, she resumed her needlework. "Very much so."

And it did. They had been made to feel most welcome. Truly cherished.

Yet still.

"What is it, sister?" Maude said gently, seeing straight through her no matter how discreet she tried to be. "You might be able to hide it from everyone else but not me. Something troubles you."

"It does not."

"It does."

She shook her head. "No."

"Yes." Maude rested her hand over Grace's this time and eyed her with concern. "Tell me."

They could sit here and do this all day, but she knew she would lose in the end, so she confessed what had been weighing on her mind for several days now. It had been a mild concern when she came here, yet it had grown. Not because she felt unwelcome but because she was more prideful than she realized.

"I cannot tell you how thankful I am to you and your husband, but I worry..." She hoped her sister did not get offended. "Is it proper for me and mine to be here, all things considered?"

"All things considered?" Maude's brow furrowed. "Whatever do you mean?"

"I mean your hospitality has been above and beyond." She swallowed back emotion at her growing discomfort. The shame she felt living off her sister. "We both know this can only last so long at my age."

While no longer in her blooming youth, she was still in her child-bearing years. Therefore, no matter how much she rejected the concept, she should look for a new husband rather than wither her days away, letting her kin pay her, and her son's, way.

"I do not see how your age plays a role in things, as you are not beholden to have another child, Grace," Maude said. "I think rather you worry about overstaying your welcome, which will never happen." As if devastated by the idea of Grace leaving, she blinked back tears. "As long as you are happy, you are always welcome. Never doubt that."

No doubt she meant it, but Grace could not help but wonder if she had misread her sister a week later when Maude and Blake hosted a dinner party. One that, ironically enough, consisted of several eligible aristocratic men.

Chapter Two

CHARLES SCOWLED AT the drip hitting his nose and glared out his once-glorious carriage window. The last thing he wanted to do was grovel at his friend Blake's feet to consider bringing his shipping business to Charles' port, but at this point, what choice did he have? He had driven his estate into the ground through grief-stricken neglect and an angry, bitter mind that had not been able to see past his woes.

When he heard what Blake was offering, though, he felt a glimmer of hope.

"Chin up, Captain," his old valet might have said if he were still around. He could almost see the merry twinkle in his eyes as he tried to remain stern. *"You are on the right track now. Mark my words, the best track."*

He could only pray. Truth told, his current track was most unpredictable, and his competition fierce if tonight's guest list was anything to go off of. He and Blake might be old friends, but that did not mean MacLauchlin would choose Charles' port for his future endeavors. If he did, however, it would mean a much-needed source of revenue for him, Newcastle, and its surrounding villages.

Blake's rather jolly butler opened the front door upon Charles' arrival. "Greetings, my lord."

He nodded once and handed his coat and hat over. "Finley."

Unlike his chilly ill-kept estate, a crackling fire warmed MacLauchlin Castle's candlelit great hall. From what he could tell, nobody else had arrived yet. Hopefully, none would, so he would not have to suffer making pleasantries.

Moreover, he reminded himself, suffer any more competition.

"Newcastle, old chap, good to see you," Blake boomed from the drawing room entrance. He grinned and waved him over. "Come join us while we await the others."

So much for him being the only attendee. If anything, all would arrive promptly. Anyone of standing with a port on or near England or Scotland's east coast would be vying for Blake's business. Where he had expected to find a competitor or two awaiting him in the drawing room, he was surprised to discover only Lady MacLauchlin and a beautiful woman dressed in black.

Where he typically cared less about his appearance, he became acutely self-aware as Maude introduced her sister, Lady Grace Howard. Lady Grace's hair was the color of spun gold, and her features exquisite. Taller than most women, she had a willowy, delicate frame with just enough curves to draw a man's eyes.

Not his, of course.

He could not recall the last time he had admired a woman. Desired her. Not since his late wife, to be sure. Why bother considering his looks? The patch over his missing left eye? The scar on his right cheek? Both were consistently disagreeable to the fairer sex.

In spite of these deformities, Grace smiled warmly. "So nice to meet you, my lord."

Where he usually found voices grating, she possessed a soft, soothing tone that agreed with him.

"You as well, my lady," he said, more gruffly than intended. But then, he was caught off guard by her. Uncomfortable in a most unusual way.

Maude urged everyone to sit on sofas that faced one another

in front of yet another welcoming fire. She and Blake sat on one. Charles and Grace, the other. Close enough to tuck a loose thread beneath his sleeve lest she notice his wardrobe was not at its best.

There had been a time when he would have known just what to say in such company. A time before the war and losing his wife, when he had been rather dashing and a practiced flirt. Nowadays, however, he was neither, so he sat quietly and tried to enjoy his drink. Blake had his own distillery, so his Scottish whisky was a cut above the rest, however illegal it may technically be. Either way, he found it difficult to focus on whisky, or anything else for that matter, with Grace sitting beside him.

He had visited MacLauchlin Castle once since Blake and Maude married and found his friend's new wife a breath of fresh air. Where most women in their circles were terribly vain and put on airs, neither applied to Maude. Instead, she was frank and lively, making a point of getting to know him where few bothered. Then again, he rarely left his estate, and when he did, he was sure to scowl at any woman who dared to come too close.

Maude, however, was not frightened off and shared much about herself, including her upbringing with her three sisters. So he knew of Grace. Like him, she had been deeply in love with her spouse. Maude also described her as a gentle spirit with a kind heart. A nature, it appeared, that had not been drained from her upon her late husband's passing.

"Ah, there you are, my dear nephew." Maude's face lit up when a boy appeared at the doorway alongside an older woman who must be his nanny. "Come say hello to our friend, Lord Newcastle, before you retire for the eve." She introduced him as Grace's son, Alexander, before patting the sofa beside her. "Sit with us for a moment, darling."

The nanny curtsied and continued on her way as Alexander gave Grace a kiss on the cheek and sat beside his aunt. Charles could tell the boy was no more comfortable in other people's company than he was. By the looks of it, he was equally withdrawn, too. Occasionally, he glanced Charles' way only to quickly avert his eyes. What child would not when presented with a monster?

Though withdrawn, Alexander clearly adored his mother. His gaze might be sad when he stared at her more often than not, but it also possessed affection and even a touch of worry if Charles was not mistaken. Might it be fear that he would lose her too? That would make sense given the boy's circumstances.

While Alexander's visit was brief, it gave him further insight into Grace's character. Especially when he viewed the love she had for her child, which was evident when compared to that of many mothers of their society who tended to thrive best with their children set aside at boarding school. There were benefits to it, of course, but he could not help but approve of Grace keeping her son close. He would have done the same if he and his wife had been fortunate enough to have children of their own.

"I know you must get to sleep soon, nephew," Maude eventually said. She stood and held out her elbow to Alexander. "So, might I escort you?"

"You may." Alexander bid everyone a good eve and was on his way with an aunt who Charles suspected intended to spoil him with a treat before she saw him to bed. Meanwhile, it seemed Blake was off to greet new arrivals, leaving him and Grace alone.

Small talk with women was as foreign to him nowadays as flirting, so it was no surprise an awkward silence fell. Both sipped their drinks, uncertain what to say before she cleared her throat and spoke, her honesty most welcome.

"You must accept my apologies, my lord." She offered him a tentative smile. "My mourning period has kept me home for some time, so I am out of practice when it comes to speaking with those such as yourself. Anyone in proper society, for that matter."

"Then we have that in common." He offered an equally tentative smile. Or at least he hoped it would appear that way, as nowadays, smiling was not his forte. "I, too, have been around proper company very little." He pointed out the obvious. "As you can see, I am unfit for those in our circles."

"You are quite blunt, my lord." Grace averted her eyes as if she feared he might be offended by her looking at him. Yet she did not shy away with her reply. "Perhaps a means to unsettle others before they unsettle you?"

Ah, equally blunt. And astute. "Perhaps."

"Then you do yourself a disservice."

In his opinion, he did himself a favor. He perked his eyebrows. "How so?"

"Need you ask?" Her gaze returned to his face. To his patch and scar. "Or do you assume everyone to whom you speak is superficial?"

"The thought has crossed my mind," he said dryly. "As I have found those of our class shallow indeed."

"All of us, then?" She narrowed her thickly-lashed, golden brown eyes. "That seems a rather broad statement when I suspect you have not met us all. As it were, you did not meet me until just now."

No, but he rather wished he had. He might not be interested in love, but conversing with someone who spoke intelligently without staring or wincing was welcome.

More welcome than he realized up until now.

"Very true. I did not meet you until just now, my lady." He considered her. "So, you argue that those of the aristocracy I have yet to meet are fine folk. Not vain or judgmental in the least."

"Good Lord, I would never claim such." She flinched. "That would make me rather naïve, would it not?"

"It would."

"Even so." She kept her gaze steady on him rather than avert her eyes again. "I think it unfair of you to assume so many of us are that atrocious."

Atrocious, was it? An apt description of how he viewed most nowadays.

"Fairness is the least of my concerns." Or so he said. In truth, its lack thereof was likely at the heart of his short range of emotions. Anger and disgust. Not just at others but himself. "Why should it be when fairness ranks rather low from what I have seen?"

"Then it seems you have lived a dim life, to be sure, my lord," she said softly. "As I have seen with my sister, Maude, fairness is crucial. But then, one would have to have a sibling born a commoner and take the time to understand her life before marrying into the Ton to see things from my vantage."

He had expected many a comeback but not that. Not actual compassion for those less fortunate than them. If one wanted to call him fortunate, nowadays. Most of his staff had been dismissed. His estate was in ruins. His beloved wife had passed. Worse still, he had borne no offspring, so there was little hope for the future of his lineage.

"While I appreciate your optimism, my lady—" he saw things clearly enough—"I cannot help but think such comes from mere sympathy rather than empathy born of actual experience, thus it mayhap be a tad naïve, after all. Defending social injustice or hard times is one thing. Living it quite another."

Her finely arched eyebrows edged together, and the corners of her mouth lowered just enough to let him know she fought a rude reply. One that he would rightly deserve, but nowadays, he knew little more than how to be blunt and direct. She, in turn, seemed able to keep her genteel nature at the forefront, yet the slight tensing of her hand on her glass spoke to the potential of a terser reply.

"I am sure you are right that living a more difficult life gives one a more thorough perspective. That is logical, good sir." She cocked her head. Her pupils flared. "And perhaps my optimism does come from sympathy, but might you not agree that a sympathetic nature is more prone to fairness? I, for one, find sympathy not the beastly falsity you clearly think it, but a much welcome perspective in those born to wealth and privilege."

"And I would tend to agree if I saw more of it."

"Said so cynically as you sit in Lord MacLauchlan's castle," she pointed out. "A highborn acquaintance who is undeniably sympathetic and most certainly fair."

He quirked the corner of his mouth. "Hence him being one of the few I call a friend, rather than an acquaintance."

"Yet someone who must surely suffer from naiveté as well, given he has no real-life experience with poverty, or *hard times*, as you call them," she pointed out. Her brows swept up. "Where, my lord, I must assume you do?"

"Why assume when it is clear?"

"There you go trying to unsettle me again."

"Are you so unsettled, then?"

"Not at all. Rather I am curious." Her voice softened. "And, as we seem to be on the topic, sympathetic."

"I fear you confuse pity for sympathy, my lady."

"Then you would be wrong." Where most women would have politely excused themselves by now, it seemed Grace was no such creature. Rather, she pressed on. "I am not one to flee when growled at, nor do I think you deserve such."

"Did I growl?" He sipped his whisky. "I rather thought our conversation polite."

"I imagine you did."

"Then it seems I very much did deserve you fleeing my presence."

She was about to reply when Maude popped her head back in and smiled. "Dinner will be served soon, so do make your way to the dining room, Lord Newcastle." Her merry gaze went to Grace. "If I might steal you for a moment, sister?"

"Of course." Grace smiled pleasantly at him as if they had just enjoyed a lovely stroll rather than a disagreeable conversation. "It was a pleasure speaking with you, my lord."

Doubtful. "You as well, my lady."

While tempted to watch her leave the room, as she had a way of drawing his eye, he focused on the fire instead. Stared into flames that tried to pull his mind back to another time. To a wicked explosion followed by smoke and death. Wails of pain. He blinked and tore his attention away lest he slip into a mood too dark for current company, an inescapable place that would ruin any chance of Blake's patronage.

That in mind, he set aside his whisky and roamed MacLauchlin Castle's familiar corridors until Blake urged him to join everyone in the dining room. He could not remember the last time he'd sat down with others to enjoy such fine fare. Everything from artichoke soup to roasted pork, flavorful vegetables, and a choice of either sherry or hock, a German white wine that suited the meal well.

Fortunately, Blake insisted he sit beside him, which put him across from Maude and Grace. He could only hope such an opportune placement meant his friend would favor his proposal above the others. While that did not mean they would talk business at the table, it did give him an opportunity to be closer than the others if MacLauchlin had a question or two about his port.

Unfortunately, the gentlemen closest to them were less willing to wait for potential questions and more forthright in painting pleasant pictures of their locations. They touted everything from coasts rich with schools of fish to other natural resources that would only complement Blake's ventures.

If that were not frustrating enough, the bloke sitting beside Grace was not shy about admiring her. It mattered not to him that she was in mourning. Why would it? Setting aside her beauty, she possessed the proper status to make her well-suited for remarrying. Not just that, but one might find it beneficial to land both Blake's money and his sister-by-marriage.

Better still, the added income she may bring.

In his opinion, she would be a fool to marry any of them. To ever marry again, for that matter. Why put herself through such when she could likely live a pleasant enough life off a portion of her late husband's estate?

Unless, of course, she believed she might love again, which seemed preposterous.

Finding love once was more than anybody could ask for. The idea that it would happen twice seemed foolish. Moreover, why risk it when illness or accident could take it away so easily? Perhaps she felt the same, considering she should have been out of mourning by now. It had been over a year and a day since her husband died, had it not?

As to be expected, the few wives in attendance kept their eyes averted from him and did not initiate a conversation. Thank God for it, too. Their topics of conversation were banal, anything but titillating. However, across the way, Grace seemed to enthrall whoever she engaged with. A lovely swan amongst the rabble. He tried not to envy them her conversation or the warm smiles she bestowed.

Or so they seemed to the untrained eye.

Truth told, he saw something else: the way her gentle laughter did not quite meet her eyes. The flicker of sadness in her gaze when she thought no one was looking. A melancholy he knew all too well. One he had battled for years to no avail. Every so often, he fancied her gaze drifted his way, but surely it was his imagination. A flicker of candlelight playing tricks on him.

"I know this eve is for business," Maude said, after they'd finished eating, "but I encourage everyone to stay on awhile after meeting with my husband." She smiled. "There will be cards and a bit of dancing, and we would so enjoy your company."

He could think of nothing more dismal but managed a cordial smile in return, grateful when the men retired for brandy, and the reason for his attendance was underway. Not just that, but he had grown tired of the simpering fools around Grace. From what he could overhear, their topics were dull, and their assumption she had not a lick of intelligence grating. Because they did assume such. He could see it in their calculating, cunning eyes. They considered her an easy target when she had presented no such character thus far.

"Come join me in my study, Charles," Blake said as they left the dining room. "I wish to speak with you alone. Catch up some before I speak with the others."

He was unsure if such a request so soon was good or bad. Did MacLauchlin mean to let him down now instead of making him suffer more needless anticipation? Rather than sit across from one another at his desk, Blake poured them whisky and urged Charles to join him in plush leather seats in front of the fire.

"You live far too close to visit so rarely." Blake considered him. "How have you been, old friend?"

By the way Blake eyed him, he knew bloody well how he fared. The key was how honest Charles would be in his response. A means, of course, to see how honest he would be in business.

Blunt and honest always.

His friend should know that by now.

"I am as I was when last we met," Charles said. "Miserable but getting by."

"Without a valet at that," Blake noted. "And a driver who serves as a footman."

"Is that so uncouth?" Because he could care less.

"In certain circles, you know it is." Blake gave him a look. "Maude and I, however, are not of those circles." He sighed. "I would say the more notable concern is how telling your circumstances have become."

"A concern that has nothing to do with the people in my village nor the workers they can provide," he cut back. "Hard workers ready and able to help new businesses flourish. A community that will compliment and make you and yours welcome on your upcoming venture."

"Ah, yes, that." Blake kept considering him in that unnerving way he had been so good at since they were boys. As though he could see right through him. "The community you have let yourself come to ruin for."

He went to deny it, but Blake spoke first and made things perfectly clear. "You need to understand something up front, old chap. Everyone here tonight is a viable candidate for my next business venture. All qualify equally." He shook his head. "So you need not pitch me on Newcastle and its surrounding boroughs. I know them and you well." He gave him a reluctant look he did not much like. "Rather, my next move will have everything to do with Lady Grace Howard and whom she chooses to marry."

Chapter Three

THE LAST THING Grace wanted to do was partake in cards and dancing, but Maude insisted she join them. How superficial it felt, though, as aristocratic wives tried to win over Maude's favor so their husbands might win Blake's money.

"Did you see Lord Newcastle?" one woman tittered from behind her fan. "Positively *horrid*." She shivered in disgust. "What was he *thinking* showing himself so openly?"

"I could not agree more," another said, fanning herself despite shivering as well. "He is brutish to look upon. Like a rogue pirate with off-putting intentions. But then he *was* a sea captain, was he not?"

"Off-putting indeed, and yes, a Royal Navy captain, I believe," another chimed in, offering her own token shiver and contradictory fan. One she used a bit too robustly. "Thank goodness his wife passed before she had to see such, though I imagine he ravished her well prior to—"

"Enough." Not concerned about propriety or wounding delicate feelings, Grace shook her head at the lot of them. "Have you no sense of decency? Lord Newcastle is a war veteran and should be treated with respect. With gratitude, for defending our beloved country. Us and our way of life." She looked from face to face. "Just imagine where we proper Englishwomen and Scotswomen would be today if Napoleon had conquered this land? Certainly not talking crassly behind our fans about those who protected our freedom at the expense of limbs, disfigurement, or both."

Though tempted to snub her nose and walk away, she would do no such thing. They could walk away, and they did. Good riddance, too. She had not missed their sort. Not for a moment. She might have refrained from speaking against them in the past for fear of offending anyone who might forgive her husband's debts, but those days were behind her.

Yet, a nagging voice reminded her they could just as easily control her son's future.

Blast it all, though. What kind of future was she thrusting Alexander into by befriending that lot? A facile and unhappy one, no doubt. Even so, as she had so recently pointed out to Lord Newcastle, they were not all like that. Just look at Maude and Blake. And Prudence and her husband, Jacob.

"Oh, thank goodness you are alone." Maude appeared out of nowhere, plunked rather than sat gracefully beside her, and spoke from behind her fan. "And I applaud how you ended up in such a state."

"You hear well, given you seem to have appeared out of thin air." She spoke behind her fan in turn. "But I am glad you decided to rejoin me as you are, by far, the most gracious, admirable woman in this room."

"Well, thank you." Maude looked at her with approval. "Although I think you are even more gracious and admirable, and I could not be more grateful."

"Truly, considering it was your guests I just offended?"

"Such offensive behavior deserves it." She eyed Grace with pride. "Again, thank you. I know Blake would have appreciated you coming to Charles' defense every bit as much as I do."

"No need to thank me." She scanned the room once again, wondering if he would appear and especially if she might engage him in yet another unusual conversation. "I see many of your husband's acquaintances have rejoined the festivities. Can we expect the same of Lord Newcastle?"

"I am afraid not." Maude sighed. "It seems after speaking with Blake alone, Charles bid us a good eve and left."

"That is too bad." She tried to hide her disappointment. While Charles had been an offensive sort, she understood his off-putting demeanor. Understood why he would push people away even though he need not. He might be scarred, but she'd found him still very handsome with his thick, dark chocolate brown hair and startling light blue eye. His patch and scar made him appear roguish, and his tall, broad-shouldered build was imposing. She had heard plenty of gossip over the past few hours about how dashing he used to be, a real catch, but she thought him rather fetching just as he was.

"It *is* too bad Charles left." Maude considered her in that big-sister way of hers. "How did you find him when we left you in the drawing room? Did you enjoy his company?"

"Not at all." Recalling the peculiar way he had made her come to attention, she thought about it. "Yet, somehow still, quite a bit."

"Indeed?" A small smile hovered on Maude's mouth. "Pray tell?"

"No, I think you should tell me how you hoped it went." Her sister should know better than to think Grace missed her telling remark. "You and Lord MacLauchlin left us alone on purpose, did you not?" She arched an eyebrow. "Perhaps playing matchmakers once more?"

"Never," Maude admonished. Her cheeks turned rosy, and her fan swung into action. "That would be most inappropriate—" she gestured loosely at Grace's black dress—"considering you have declared yourself still in mourning even though the properly allotted grieving time has passed."

"I am allowed to be in mourning as long as I wish, Maude," she reminded her. "The rest of my life if I so choose."

"But will you?" Maude's eyebrows pinched before she pressed her lips together in regret and shook her head. "I am sorry, dear sister. You must forgive me. If it is your wish to mourn William until the bitter end, I understand."

She frowned. "Bitter?"

"Is there a better word?" Maude hung her head just enough to continue looking properly apologetic. "Again, I am so sorry. Mourning and staying true to your one true love until the end is most admirable." She shrugged a little. "Even if he is no longer here to cherish such devotion."

For a moment, Grace found herself unable to think. The pain of losing William crashed over her anew in a tsunami of sadness and yet just as quickly, it left her. Roiling away, leaving her breathless and trembling. What Maude said was true. William wasn't coming back and yes, he was not able to witness her devotion. But even so, she couldn't allow her sister to ride roughshod over her or discount her loss.

"Maude," she exclaimed. "You go too far." *Unless...did Maude want her married off and out of her home as soon as possible?* "Is this about me overstaying my welcome here after all?"

"Goodness, no!" Maude's eyes widened. "I would keep you and Alexander here indefinitely if I had my way, as would Blake..." She struggled with her words. "Yet, I know..."

"Know what?" she prompted when her sister trailed off.

"I know you suffer from damning—" Maude cleared her throat—"I mean *admirable* pride." She wrapped her fingers with Grace's. "You have since you were a little girl, and that has not changed. No matter what I say, I know you will only stay on here so long. That you are already contemplating what you must do so you do not feel like a burden despite the wealth you see around you. The roof that would gladly stay over your head to the very end."

Maude did know her well because she was right.

It might be the last thing she wanted to do, but she and Alexander could not stay on here indefinitely. It was too much to ask, which left her only one option: Marry again. Better still, marry someone who could provide for her because she came with so little.

"And you thought Lord Newcastle a good choice for me?" Grace might frown, but she was admittedly curious. "A man who, while admirable for what he did for our country, is quite miserable. Angry at all from what I could see. Hateful, if given half the chance. A man who clearly wants nothing to do with people, let alone marriage."

"Well, yes, that does describe him quite well."

"It describes him entirely."

"Yet still." Maude fiddled with her fan and sighed again, quite crestfallen all of a sudden. "I think we both know it is all for show. He is bitter about his wounds and still devastated over the loss of his late wife." Her lower lip wobbled when her gaze drifted back to Grace's face. "Much like you, I would say. He did so love her, and I thought perhaps…"

"What?" she wondered. "That we would find love amid our mutual heartache? Understand one another as no one else could? That I would be able to overlook his obstinate, callous attitude because he suffers as I do?"

"Well, yes." Maude cocked her head. "Is that such unreasonable thinking?"

"When one considers there is a boy equally wounded attached to all this, yes, it is." She tilted her head as well. "Did you and Lord MacLauchlin keep such in mind? Consider what it might be like for Alexander to have a father like Lord Newcastle?"

"Yes, because he had a child," Maude blurted before she put a hand over her mouth and rounded her eyes again. "Please forget I said that," she murmured through her fingers.

A chill went through her. "I will not." She gently reached to grasp Maude's hand and lower it from her face. "What happened?"

"So, you do not know?" she said softly, leaning closer even though nobody was nearby. "You did not hear?"

"Hear what?" While she had heard Charles was a war hero who became an uncouth beast after his injuries, she knew nothing of his private life.

"His late wife, God rest her soul, lost her life and that of their baby's during childbirth," Maude confessed sadly. "They say it was why he went off to war in the first place. That he no longer cared if he lived or died."

"Whether that was the case or not, best you never repeat such, as it is in poor taste," she said gently, saddened by the information. It did explain a lot, though. "I am so sorry to hear of his considerable loss. I cannot even imagine."

"Can you not, then, sister?" Maude said just as gently.

"No," she whispered, struggling to find her voice. Unwilling to look at the entirety of her losses too closely. "And I beg you never to ask me that again."

Before Maude could respond, Grace bid her goodnight and left, needing the sanctity of her bedroom like she needed to breathe. An escape from old memories that were better left in the past.

"Are you well?" Catlin asked as she helped her undress a short while later. She clearly knew better than to address her as 'my lady' right now.

"I am," she managed, desperate to crawl beneath the covers and lose herself in a good cry. "Thank you."

"You say such, but you are not well at all." Catlin urged her to sit on the bed and crouched in front of her. "Tell me. What is it?"

"We share more than one thing in common." She bit back tears. "And it is something no two people should share."

Catlin's brows furrowed before she seemed to understand. "You refer to Lord Newcastle and the child he lost, yes?"

"I do." Having lost a child early in pregnancy before Alexander, she frowned. "How did you know?"

"You know full well how." Catlin looked skyward before squeezing Grace's hand. "Gossip below stairs is just as bad as above stairs. It seems this is only the second time he has appeared in public for the better part of three years, so tongues were bound to be wagging."

"Three *years*?" she said weakly, yet again saddened for him. Seeing what she could have become in him had she not left her home. Had she stayed on like she wanted. "How awful."

"Truly." Catlin cupped her cheek. "What can I do for you, friend? Would you like to sit up and talk? I can fetch some tea. Or perhaps have a bath drawn?"

"No, I think just rest."

Fortunately, Catlin knew better than to press the issue and saw Grace well settled. Or so she thought. In truth, she never really relaxed. Instead, she tossed and turned, eager to escape her restless thoughts.

"Then get up and make use of it," her younger sister, Abby, would say if she were here. "Live outside the doom and gloom you refuse to release yourself from. Do something I never can."

What to do, though? How to escape?

"Is it not safe to say you are already free?" Abby would counter. "Now, take the next step, because we both know you cannot live off Maude's hospitality forever. Neither of us could, despite how much she might be determined to keep us."

She was right. It was not who they were.

Who *she* was.

This left her only one course of action. Whether she liked it or not or even had much to offer a man, she must find a suitable husband who could provide her son the life he deserved, especially a good education and a solid future. Her own wants must be set aside. So she sat at the small desk in her room and penned a message to be delivered to Maude first thing in the morning.

A letter that had her sister sweeping into her room at the crack of dawn.

"I *knew* you would do this." Maude sat beside Grace on the bed. "I knew you would want to leave me." She wagged Grace's letter in the air. "I just knew it!"

Grace tried to get a word in edgewise, but Maude barely

paused to breathe.

"So now what?" Just like when they were children, she lay beside Grace, crossed her arms over her chest, and jutted her chin. "You are going to marry some miserable royal that will take you away from all the love you and Alexander have here? Steal you away from such a wonderful future at MacLauchlin Castle?"

"I believe you saw this coming last night, sweet sister. Hence Lord Newcastle." She rolled on her side, braced up on an elbow, and fiddled with one of Maude's many stubborn curls. "But, yes, as my letter conveyed, I must do just that." She searched her sister's eyes and blinked back tears. "Surely, you see that? Surely you understand we cannot live off your goodwill forever?"

Maude frowned and wiped away her own tears. "Yet you would live off the goodwill of another?"

"Again, was that not your intention when you left me alone with Lord Newcastle?"

The corners of Maude's mouth inched up. "Did he catch your fancy that much, then?"

"I never said that." She had, though. Not for marital purposes, of course, but for kindred life experiences, as it turned out. Perhaps an ally in all the disaster that had been hers. The ruin she still tried to navigate free from. "I have no interest in marrying Lord Newcastle, and I can assure you, he has no interest in marrying me either." She made a gesture as though slicing the idea away. "The two of us would never pair well. It would be a disaster."

"How could you possibly know that?" Before she could respond, Maude waved it off. Done with the possible mournful departure of her sister, she sat up and grinned, her smile so sunny one would think she had not shed a tear moments before. "If you are so determined to marry and shove off, I propose an idea. One you can back out of at any time. In fact, I would prefer it."

"And what is this idea?" she said tentatively because one never knew when it came to Maude and her well-meaning schemes.

"A ball." Sensing Grace was taking the bait, Maude's eyes went round as saucers, and her grin blossomed into a wide smile. "One Blake and I have come to coin a second-chance ball, considering he and I fell in love at a ball in this very castle. Then, Prudence first fell in love with her Jacob at a ball once again, in this castle." She shook her head, suddenly most rueful and serious. "Of course, this ball will have less to do with romance but more to see you and Alexander happy if you should wish it. It will allow you the chance to choose who you marry next." She gestured at Grace. "As it should be."

"Even though I am the prize."

"That is right." Maude's eyes rounded even wider when she realized what she had said. "No, not the prize but, but—"

"But, what?" Grace saw this for what it was, and it did not make sense. "A bride coming to them with little more than the title with which she went into her former marriage and a dowry far more meager than they might imagine? Not just that, but a son they would need to care for as well. One that tends to need more attention than most."

"And that has been taken into account," Maude said without quite meeting her eyes.

"Taken into account?" Her shoulders grew tight. "How so?" When her sibling flew to Grace's armoire and rifled through her array of black dresses, Grace followed. "Maude?"

"Yes?" her sister answered absently.

"How has my second-chance ball, as you call it, taken into account my lack of suitable income? Two mouths to feed rather than one? A proper education for a young boy? A dowry that is meager indeed for a woman that is no longer in her blooming youth?"

"Well, we were hoping you might reconsider that dowry."

"Reconsider?" She shook her head, confused, before she realized her sister and Blake intended to contribute.

"Absolutely not." How embarrassing. "I will not. *You* will not."

Maude seemed to gather herself before she squared her

shoulders and looked at Grace like never before. "We will. It is done." She stood up a tad straighter. "William's debts have been paid off in full and replaced in your dowry."

Surely not. Overwhelmed by nausea, she sank onto the edge of the bed.

"Oh, dear." Maude sat beside her and clasped Grace's suddenly shaky hands. "Please do not be upset. We meant no harm. Only ever the best for you, Grace. Surely you know that. Understand it."

"Understand?" she said weakly, ashamed. "All I understand is that I..." *Failed? Lost track of William's spending? Underestimated how bad his gambling addiction had become?* All of the above, it seemed. Even so, she refused to have his good name slandered, so she glared at her sister when Maude was the last person who deserved it. "Who else knows because surely you are why I still had a roof over my head after he passed?"

"Only those to whom he owed money," Maude said gently. "They are all behind you now. Your future is secure."

Grace did not need to ask to understand what that meant. "You are not my mother, nor is Blake my father, Maude. Therefore, you do not need to provide a dowry." She shook her head. "It is foolish and unheard of at this point."

"The point being your age, yes? Well, our parents have already passed, so you can look at this however you like, but considering I am your oldest sibling, I see things from one vantage only." Maude tilted Grace's chin until she had no choice but to look at her. "To my way of thinking, I am responsible for you and Alexander's well-being. More than that, I would consider it a privilege. An honor." She searched Grace's eyes. "Have you not seen that in your time here? How much I adore you both? Blake and I adore you?"

"I have, and I could not be more thankful."

What to say? Feel? It seemed surreal knowing her secrets were not secret at all. She was not the epitome of the elegant well-bred lady she fancied herself. Instead, she felt laid bare and not notable enough to be recommended in proper society. She did not care much for the Haute Ton, but she *did* care a great deal for her son's future in it. That he might only ever be admired, not just by them but by all. If they slandered him, opportunities might very well be denied him. Doors could be shut in his face.

"Be that as it may," Grace continued, struggling with her dignity and, yes, her pride, "What you did is too much. If that were not enough, what you hope to accomplish with this second-chance ball will cost money, too."

"Money we will willingly spend if you agree to it." Maude held her hands again and smiled. "Money you can always reimburse in the future if you wish."

"Assuming my future husband would honor such," she said softly. "As he would control everything."

"He would." Maude dared to offer a small grin. "If you choose poorly."

She frowned, unsettled by the thought but, at the same time, intrigued. "So this second-chance ball, as you call it, would not be about him choosing me but the other way around?" A considerably different concept than her coming out ball years ago. "Truly?"

"Naturally." Maude grew rather grave and shook her head. "I would have it no other way in my castle with my sister." She eyed Grace curiously. "So, what do you think? Should we begin planning?"

"Would it not be more frugal to simply make it a dinner party?"

"Perhaps, but what fun would there be in that?" Maude's grin returned. "Besides, I do so love hosting balls here."

Grace thought about it for a moment. Could she do this? Was she truly ready? Unlikely. But what choice did she have? Because she did intend to pay her sister back, which she could not accomplish on her own.

So, her decision was fairly simple.

"Then I suppose we should begin planning," she finally said. "Where to start, though?"

Maude's dubious gaze returned to Grace's armoire and her row of black dresses. "Need you ask?"

Chapter Four

One month later.

NOT FOR THE first time, Charles debated whether he should have his driver turn the carriage around. Was this a good idea? Could he woo Grace, never mind convince her to marry him? The idea seemed far-fetched, but what choice did he have? Blake had not only provided her a handsome dowry but would bring his substantial shipping business to the port of whomever she married so Maude could visit with her regularly.

So, even though winning Grace over seemed impossible, he had to try for the sake of his community. And while he could think of nothing worse than remarrying, he could admit she was a better option than most. That in mind, best that he tried to win her favor and suspected he knew just how to go about it.

Logically and without fuss.

Or so he assumed that was the best option, given he surmised she wanted marriage no more than he. Otherwise, why wear her mourning clothes for so long? Suffice it to say, he did not turn his carriage back but pressed on, arriving at MacLauchlin Castle along with several others.

"Hello, Finley." He thanked MacLauchlin's butler when he took his coat and hat and formally announced his esteemed arrival as the Earl of Newcastle in a loud, carrying voice. Ignoring the uncomfortable glances he received, he took in the festive ambiance, from the candlelit chandeliers to the delicacies and champagne served by sharply presented staff. Music already drifted from the ballroom. "I see the festivities are well underway."

"They are, my lord," Finley said. "Though we still await the guest of honor."

He no sooner said it than Grace appeared at the top of the stairs on Blake's arm, and murmurs rippled through the room. Charles had expected to find her just as beautiful as when last they met but had not realized how breathtaking she would be out of her mourning clothes. Nor that he would feel an unusual stirring at the sight of her.

One he had not felt in far too long.

Grace's golden locks were swept up in an elegant bun, and silky curls framed her heart-shaped face. A lovely sage green dress complimented her lithe frame and plumped up the soft mounds of her cleavage. Delicate emeralds dripped from her ears, and a matching emerald necklace wrapped her slender neck. While more than tempted to steal her way, he held back for now. Intended to go about things differently. Preferably without stepping foot on the dance floor.

He had not danced with another since his late wife and had no desire to start now.

"Ah, welcome, Lord Newcastle." Maude melted out of the crowd and smiled warmly. "I am so glad you accepted our invitation." She asked a servant to fetch him a glass of whisky and considered him. "Might I assume you are here for Grace's hand?"

"Was that not the reason for the invitation?"

"It was." She was no more put off by his bluntness than her sister. "Even so, I am glad you accepted. Given your hasty departure last time, I was not sure you would."

He had left soon after learning what Blake intended because he had no intention of taking another wife. Not ever. Not even for the betterment of his people.

At least, that had been his initial reaction.

"I would rather Grace not know about Blake's promise to her future betrothed regarding his business venture," Maude said softly, surprising him on several fronts. "At least not right away."

"You say that as if you assume I will be the one keeping it from her."

"Considering you want marriage no more than she does, I imagine you will." She eyed him in a rather wise way which proved just how observant she actually was. "Or have I miscalculated that you did not know she felt that way? That you intended to use it to your advantage this very night?"

Well done, Maude. "Would it be so wrong of me?"

"Not at all." She tossed him a pointed look. "I would think it rather prudent."

Before he could reply, she smiled at someone who had just walked in, bid him farewell, and drifted into the crowd. So, there it was. Permission from her kin if he did not know better. Did that mean he already had Blake's business?

Not necessarily, but it was promising.

He scanned his surroundings and saw no sign of Grace, so he made his way into the ballroom, sure to keep to the shadows and avoid conversations. Not that he need worry, given people tended to steer clear of him anyway.

Where had she gone? He thought he would find her on the dance floor swept up in some hopeful's arms, but she was nowhere to be seen. So he made his way from room to room, looking for her. When he could not locate her, he started down several hallways until he finally spied her alone in one of the smaller corridors staring at a portrait.

"Lady Howard." He bowed at the waist. "Apologies for disturbing you."

"Lord Newcastle." She did not seem startled in the least. Rather she appeared to expect him and curtsied. "What brings you this way?"

"I think that would be obvious."

"Then I would think my reasons for being here alone in a rather desolate hall admiring a couple is no more equally obvious."

He considered the picture she had been looking at. Or, better put, seemed lost within. It was of the Duke of Argyll and his late wife. The very duke who had ended up marrying her sister, Prudence. He had been deeply in love with his former wife before he lost her and just as in love with his current wife if rumor held true.

"You wanted me to follow you here." He disregarded the strange warmth in his chest that he might be right. That Grace might be as forward-thinking as him. "You wanted me to find you admiring this portrait."

"I did." Her gaze lingered on the painting a moment longer before she looked his way again. "Why did you leave so quickly last time you were here?"

"Why do you think?"

"Let us not do that," she said softly. "Let us not banter and be direct. I must admit, I rather depended on you for that."

"So, you knew I would come tonight." Because he had sent no reply to his invitation.

"I had hoped."

He ignored a surge that it might be for all the wrong reasons. Or, as most might see it, the right reasons. Either way, if she wanted him to be direct, he would. Preferred it, actually.

Yet, he remembered what Maude had requested and would honor it for now.

"I left because Lord MacLauchlin was unable to commit to what it was I desired from him," he said. "I returned tonight because I need your dowry, and I think we can be equally beneficial to one another." He glanced from the portrait to her. "Which leads us back to why you led me to this spot. You wanted me to find you admiring love lost. To understand that you suffer such and have no intention of loving again."

If he was not mistaken, she had been prepared to propose

marriage between them before he even decided to come tonight.

"I did lead you here on purpose, and you are right." She met his gaze directly. "I desire to suffer love again no more than you, correct?"

"Correct."

"Nor do I wish to suffer the duties that come with becoming a wife." Grace swallowed and squared her shoulders as if going into battle. "Not with a stranger and not with you." She gestured between them. "To that end, I propose we serve our mutual interests. You, my dowry, and me, that Alexander and I might not take advantage of my sister and Lord MacLauchlin's goodwill for our remaining days." She shook her head once. "It is too much to ask of them, and I will not do it."

So, pride it was. Good, because he knew that beast well. "I understand."

"Do you?"

"More than you can imagine."

"Good." She eyed him warily. "On that, we are settled, but there is more. Something you must understand first."

He nodded for her to go on when she hesitated.

"My son is unwell." Grace clasped her hands in front of her and stood up straighter still. Notched her chin as though ready to defend Alexander if need be. "He suffers from hay fever, and I am afraid it can be difficult at times." She paused a moment as if gathering herself. "His breathing can become hindered, so I prefer him in my constant company. He might be getting older, but still. Right now, it is best for an adult to help him, if need be, meaning Mrs. Catlin and Mr. Hew must stay on indefinitely. A permanent part of the household, if you will."

He was not sure what caught him more off guard. How the pain she tried to hide made him feel or the worry he experienced that Alexander suffered.

"How difficult does his breathing become?" he said before he could stop himself, hearing the concern in his own voice. After all, how much difficulty must one child overcome in his life?

Between losing his father and his illness, it seemed a bit much.

"Very difficult." Grace blinked a little too fast, as though fighting emotion but kept her gaze steady on his face. She did not shy away from what needed saying. "When a particularly bad fit comes upon him, he can hardly breathe at all. It is as if..." She paused again, gathering herself once more. "It is as if someone strangles him, and if I were honest, it can be quite terrifying. So whatever path I take after this night, whatever direction I go, it must be in Alexander's best interest with a promise that he will be well cared for."

He did not need to think twice. Dowry or not, he would find the funds to keep Alexander well. "Of course, he will be. You have my word."

Her gaze lingered on his eyes as if she were trying to see just how honest he was before she finally spoke. "You mean that, do you not? Truly mean it."

"Very much so."

"Then I thank you—" Grace nodded once in acknowledgment and eyed him curiously—"and with that, I believe we have come to an agreement?" Her attention drifted back to the painting. "That will never be us. Cannot." She looked at him again. "As I am as devoted to my late husband as you are to your late wife."

"Indeed." However perfect the arrangement, something felt off about it, and he could not fathom what. "So, how would you like to proceed this evening?"

"I would like things to seem genuine enough to keep rumors from getting back to Alexander," Grace said. "He might be quiet nowadays, but he is smart. I will not have him think I conceded to an unwanted marriage for the sake of his health." She considered him for a moment, clearly hesitant about how honest she should be before continuing. "I will also not have those of our society look down on you any more than they already do. You do not deserve such gossip."

"I see." He arched an eyebrow and reminded her of their

initial conversation. "For you are nothing if not sympathetic."

She arched a brow right back. "And here, based on your very own words, I thought it was pity."

"*Touché.*" Not offended by her reasoning, he tipped an imaginary top hat. "So again, how would you like to proceed, my lady?"

"I would think arm-in-arm." She held out her elbow. "Then perhaps a dance or two, even though I suspect neither of us much wants to."

"You would suspect right." Yet he slipped his arm into hers, and they made their way back toward civilization, if one could call such a gathering civil. "Might it not be enough just to be seen together like this? Perhaps a smile here or there to make it all seem genuine?"

"It very well could be enough," she conceded. "But if we are to truly do away with my pity, as it were, might it not seem logical I would require a turn or two on the dance floor? That I should seem quite taken by you?"

"I would think it rather over the top." He could not help a wry grin, though. "That it might seem unbelievable, all things considered."

"Because the idea that I would be attracted to you is obscene?"

"Is it not?"

"I think rather it might seem that way," she said softly. "Then again, I am merely sympathetic, not empathetic. A voice you find pitying. Not just because I have not lived the life of a commoner as you pointed out when last we met, but I imagine because I have not suffered so greatly in war like you."

"Did I say all that, then?"

"More or less."

What was that scent she wore? Something subtle and flowery. "Then it seems your memory serves you well."

"It was not that long ago, my lord."

Was it not? He had felt the month rather stretched.

"I think perhaps for now, so all seems on the up and up," she went on, "we keep with being blunt, as I quite prefer it, but set aside talk of all else. Be it sympathy, empathy, pity, or otherwise."

"Were we not having fun with it?"

"Not in the least." Her look was probably better than he deserved. "It was but a means for you to challenge me, as I suspect you have challenged many since wartime. To scare me away as I do not doubt you would any and all."

"One needs them to approach first for me to scare them off."

"So self-pity, is it?"

"And here I thought that was one of the words we would not use anymore."

"That was before I realized just how much you applied it to yourself."

He bit back a smile when he would typically be inclined to scowl. "Somehow, my lady, I suspect—"

"There you two are." Maude smiled broadly at them when she again appeared out of what seemed like thin air. Her gaze swept over their linked arms before her smile grew broader still. "How nice to find you enjoying one another's company."

"Indeed." Grace smiled warmly at Charles. "We are so happy to cross paths again as we quite enjoy one another's company."

He ignored the strange feeling she had a way of invoking and worked at a smile, too. "I could not agree more."

"Might you join us in the ballroom, then?" Maude asked.

Grace's lovely smile never faltered. "We would love to, as we were hoping to get in a turn or two together."

As though that was not quite what she expected to hear, Maude blinked several times before she clasped her hands in delight. "I can think of nothing better." She glanced between them much like a child who came upon an unexpected treat before she vanished as quickly as she had come, tossing over her shoulder, "I shall see you there!"

"You do understand what she is about, yes?" Undaunted by Maude's behavior, Grace glanced at him in bemusement. "What she and Lord MacLauchlin fancy themselves?"

"I have heard rumors," he confessed while they continued strolling. He had not had a woman on his arm since his late wife and found it more distracting than he was willing to admit. "Matchmakers, yes?"

"Yes." She gave him a warning look. "And successful ones at that."

"Because of your sister, Prudence, and the Lord of Argyll."

"Somehow, I am not surprised you know that, as Maude does love to chat." They made their way into the first crowded room, and gazes turned their way. Curious eyes met by frowns of confusion hidden behind fans. "But yes, and best you keep it in mind going forward."

"So that I, again, present the proper picture of adoration?"

"To Maude and Blake?" She chuckled behind her fan as if flirting with him. "Dear Lord, no. So that you do not fall victim to them thinking they see more than actually exists between us. If that happens, they will only try to push us together more robustly."

He could just imagine. A little too vividly, at that. And it made him feel defensive for no reason other than he did not hate the concept on the spot. "That would be unfortunate."

"Agreed," she said a little too quickly. Enough to draw his gaze even though her attention was on those they passed. He could care less about granting this pompous lot a pleasant smile, but Grace seemed to think otherwise because she did just that. Over and over as she kept him close.

So close, he wondered if this was all for show.

Especially when he swore, he felt her tremble.

"We need not do this, my lady." He worried about her state because he understood it. Knew how difficult this was. "We can see through our agreement without—"

"No," she said softly, smiling at another who did not disguise his bafflement over her current company. "I will not have Alexander confused when the time comes."

Honestly, he did not see the boy caring whether she loved her next husband or not. To his mind, he would likely prefer the latter. That is when it occurred to him this had to do with more than her son. If he were not mistaken, this had to do with himself.

She had meant what she said about not liking how people treated him.

He saw it, too, when he looked more closely at her smiling at those in passing. Saw her the way he had when they first met. Past the pleasantries and politeness. Past all of it to the tension in her jawline. The delicate vein pulsing in her neck that had not been there moments before. The way she challenged all gazes with a flicker of defiance.

Sweetly masked rage if he did not know better.

"You seem upset," he said softly enough that they would not be overheard.

"Do I?" She smiled at another in passing. "Because I feel quite content."

"So now we have not only ceased certain words but stopped being honest with one another?" he wondered. "When just minutes ago you declared you preferred us being blunt."

"Did I say all that?"

"With nary a stutter."

"I see."

"Do you?" They entered the next room. While she kept smiling at others, he did not bother. "Because I find myself quite baffled."

"Well, you should not." Grace smiled and batted her lashes at him as if they exchanged witty banter, and she found him utterly captivating. "As I stated, we are to be taken with one another."

"Courting then?" While tempted to snarl at a particularly bold look of disgust from a chap, he nodded politely instead. "Courting when such would make sense to no one despite your good intentions?"

"Courting when they very much should because are you not a catch, my lord?" She stopped and looked at him when they reached the doorway to the ballroom. Looked at him with a tilt to her chin that he recognized as stubbornness. "Our plans aside, I cannot tolerate this a moment longer."

He frowned. "Tolerate what?"

"Them." She shocked him when she stood on her tiptoes, pulled his scarred cheek down, and kissed it gently before whispering in his ear. "So let us show them what fools they are. Every last one of them."

Chapter Five

SHE MIGHT PRESENT a strong, determined front, but Grace had been terrified since she approved this second-chance ball, as Maude called it. Everything had seemed out of her control since she decided the only way to satisfy her blasted pride was to remarry. From Maude having more vibrant dresses made for her to castle preparations.

"I have made a grave mistake," she had said to Catlin as she helped dress her earlier. "I should not be doing this. I can find another way." She wrung her hands and frowned at the green dress she'd just put on for the ball, the first color outside of black she had worn in far too long. Although she had fought Maude on wearing this shade, her sister was insistent, reminding her that it used to be her favorite color because it complimented her creamy skin tone and blond hair so well. "What was I thinking going along with this? Letting my sister know that I would be remarrying, to begin with?" Blinking back tears, she frowned at her friend. "I am not ready for this. Will *never* be ready for this."

"Yet here you are." Catlin looked at her with calm affection. In a matronly way, which broached little room for debate. "You might not be ready for the next step, but you are most certainly ready to leave. You have a plan, and I think it is a good one. The only one to satisfy all aspects of what you want next, Grace. How you hope to move forward."

"What if Lord Newcastle does not accept my proposal? What if I am wrong about him?" She pressed her hand to her chest. "Worse yet, what if he does not accept Maude and Lord MacLauchlin's invitation? If—"

"No more ifs or whatnots, my dear friend." Catlin added earrings to Grace's ensemble before cupping her cheek. "You made a decision, and I think it wise from its conception to its finish." With a shrug and a *We Can Handle This* attitude, she said what Grace needed to hear. "If Lord Newcastle does not arrive, then you must look to your next candidate."

"Of which there are none."

"Nevertheless." Catlin draped a delicate necklace of sparkling emeralds around Grace's neck without her gaze ever leaving her face. "You will expand your thinking if you must. Take the time to find the man who expects nothing but your dowry, for surely there must be a few."

"Or all," she muttered dryly, glancing in the mirror. "I am not in my blooming youth anymore, so perhaps you are right, and I worry when I should not. Maybe I need just find the right gentleman, present my offer, and things will go smoothly indeed."

"It could very well be."

"Yet we both know it will not." She sank onto the seat in front of her vanity and stared at her reflection. It had been a long time since she needed to depend on her appearance. Years since she had felt beautiful simply because of the appreciation in a man's eyes. "It needs to be the Earl of Newcastle. He is the only one I have faith in when it comes to Alexander."

Once she had accepted the idea of a second-chance ball and Maude updating her wardrobe, she'd become focused on him as the best option for a husband who would demand nothing of her. He would have no interest in falling in love again and might very well agree not to consummate their marriage.

So, she had made a point of learning more about him.

Mostly, that meant asking Catlin to see what she could discover below stairs and learn she did. More than Grace ever could have anticipated. As she knew, Charles had lost his beloved wife and unborn babe to childbirth, but his story grew more heart-wrenching from there. First, the obvious loss he suffered that caused him to go off to war, then those upon his return.

It seemed he had fallen into a deep melancholy that led to neglect; not of those around him but that of his fishing and shipping businesses. Many claimed he would not venture from his estate to see to things. Instead, he sold off precious heirlooms to keep food in their bellies and roofs over the heads of those under his employ. He had apparently sold nearly everything to keep the villagers and their families afloat.

In short, while he was well-liked by all in Newcastle and its surrounding villages, they worried over him terribly. He had been an astute businessman at one time, an earl that would see them thrive, but it seemed that between losing his family and being maimed in the war, the life had been drained from him.

The will to live, some said.

So why was he such a good choice to marry? To trust her son's wellbeing with? For those very reasons. In fact, the more gossip she heard about Charles, the more convinced she became about his suitability. He would not want love and likely agree to bypass the intimate details that went along with it. Moreover, he would take her dowry and care for others before himself. Some might say it could very well be his villagers over her and her son, but somehow, she doubted that. Then there was Maude and Blake's good opinion of him. She could not imagine them wanting to make a match of her and Charles if he were not a good man.

"If you have faith in Lord Newcastle, then so do I." Catlin locked gazes with her in the mirror. "You know that."

"I do. Unequivocally and again, I cannot help but wonder why." She frowned and shook her head, baffled but still somehow drawn. "His deeds have been good if not self-destructive, but still."

"Indeed, they have, yet passion remains in your voice when you speak of him, and that is what matters most." Catlin wrapped a light shawl around Grace's shoulders. "Because it is nothing less than faith you place in him. Trust."

"Based on little more than what you have learned," she reminded.

"No." Her friend looked at her affectionately. "Based on how you responded to what I have learned." She cupped Grace's cheeks. "More so, how you spoke of your first meeting with him. How clearly you saw his emotional wounds over his physical. How angry you were at how people treated him."

"I *was* angry," she granted.

"And I could not love you more for it."

"I love you too." She blinked back tears. "Thank you for all of this. For coming here. Carrying on. For loving Alexander so much. *Me* so much."

"No need to thank me, foolish girl." Catlin pointed in the mirror at Grace. "Just thank her. Trust her. Do what she feels is right tonight."

"Yes?"

"Yes."

So she did, yet again wondering if her decision to propose to Charles was the right one as she headed downstairs on Blake's arm. Would he even make an appearance? She would not blame him if he did not. Understood it more than he could possibly know. Thus, she felt tremendous relief when she spied him in the great hall.

He was here.

He had come.

"Might we go into the ballroom?" Blake had asked after announcing her. His tone was soft and far too knowing when he glanced at her. "Or were you hoping to go your own way first, my lady?"

"A bit of time to acclimate would be most welcome, my lord."

Blake glanced from Charles to her and nodded. "Of course."

What she intended to do was a brazen, unorthodox thing, but rumor had it this castle was rife for it. More than that, this was her solution. Safety when some might claim it was the very opposite. That the leap she took now was foolish by far. Either way, she made her way through the crowd and fake, wanting smiles of ingenuine gentlemen to the sparsely candlelit corridor of one of her favorite paintings in the castle.

If she was right about him, Charles would follow her. He would find this meeting of the minds preferable to all the pomp. Better still, he would already know how little competition he faced.

That she needed a false marriage every bit as much as he did.

Nonetheless, that did not stop her from holding her breath when she stopped in front of the portrait of the Duke of Argyll and his former wife. In front of the man her sister had fallen so much in love with. Would Charles come? Or would he end up fleeing like he had that first night? Because he had. As fast as he could when he thought his battle was already lost.

Yet he did not tonight.

Instead, he appeared like a phantom caught in the shadows of the hallway until he was beside her. Then, just as she imagined he might, he was ready. Here for this. Seemed to understand just as she did that marrying was their best option. There existed no romantic proposal, just witty words. No loving gazes but a mutual understanding and perhaps even ease that love need not be part of them moving forward together. Therefore, she had thought to skip all the fuss of the night and simply go to Maude and Blake and tell them how it would go.

But something had overtaken her when she walked down those stairs.

When she realized Charles had actually come.

More so, when she spoke with him. The same thing that had overtaken her when those foolish women had been so cruel speaking about him a month ago. Not only an urge to set them straight again but a need to push past the coldness in Charles' gaze and the tightness of his square jaw. A veil of protection if she did not know better.

A barrier that defended a deep hurt these shallow people could not see.

So rather than dance, she drifted into the crowd and down a hallway. She had known Charles would follow and wanted him to find her where he had. Needed to make sure she had been right about him, and she was. Saw it clearly in the way he looked at the Duke of Argyll's portrait with his former wife. The flash of pain on his face she knew nobody else would see. How could they when he allowed no one close and with good reason?

Society's behavior was awful.

She had found Charles quite handsome during their first encounter, and his evening finery only accentuated it. Honestly, it amazed her that more women did not see how attractive he truly was.

Then again, that was not entirely true, was it?

The women a month ago might have seemed disgusted by him, yet she had caught their flushed cheeks. Saw how they had fanned themselves with too much zest. They might have wanted to convince each other he was a beastly monster, but something told her they would not be opposed to a secret rendezvous with him. A dabble on the dark side, so to speak.

And it frustrated her to no end.

To the point she was determined to show them all he deserved better. He need not be hidden away to know and enjoy him because there was clearly a caring man beneath Charles' rough exterior. Someone likely starved for company whether he realized it or not.

So, while yes, she wanted Alexander to think their relationship was genuine, she also wanted to show the Ton that Charles was worth more than sneers. With that in mind, she determined they would not skip courting altogether but make a show of it.

Or at least share a dance or two.

She was unsure what she expected when a waltz conveniently played after kissing him on the cheek, but it was not that he would be so graceful sweeping her onto the dance floor. Nor that they would move so well together. That dancing with a man would come so naturally when she never thought it would again. He did make it surprisingly easy, though.

"You dance very well, my lord," she said, surprised to find herself rather breathless. But then, she had become aware of him in a most unexpected way. Not just because of his clean, masculine scent but because of his proximity. The heat and strength of his body.

"As do you, my lady," he said, his tone more guttural than before, if she were not mistaken.

She meant to respond but felt tongue-tied as their gazes held. Her heart seemed to flutter in her chest, and her breath caught. Startled by the sensation, by an attraction she had not anticipated, she nearly lost her footing, but fortunately, he led so well that she kept moving. Where she had meant to stop after one or two dances, three flew by before she realized it. If that were not enough, she was rather disappointed when they retired from the dance floor.

"Do you think they looked that stunned the whole time?" he said as they linked arms and strolled into the great hall.

"Stunned?" she said, not thinking clearly in the least.

"Yes, stunned."

She only then realized he referred to those who had watched them dance. The incredulous looks following in their wake. Women gossiped behind their fans. Men seemed baffled, or frustrated.

"Truth be told, I had not noticed until you mentioned it." She issued him a small smile. "But yes, I think them rather stunned and could not care less."

"Nor could I." He shrugged and thanked a servant who delivered them drinks. Her, claret, and he, whisky by the looks of it. "But alas, it is to be expected."

"Yet it should not be."

"No, but I am afraid such is the world in which we live, Lady Howard."

"Then, may we see it change soon." She tipped her glass to his. "Until such occurs, here is to shocking them even further." Where she had meant by dancing and being seen together, she blushed when she realized how forward that sounded. "Of course, I mean by marrying."

"Of course, my lady." He tapped his glass against hers. "Whatever else would you mean?"

While some might misinterpret his tone as flirtatious, the sudden wariness in his gaze contradicted any confusion. Or so it seemed. Must be. Whatever she had felt on the dance floor had to have been her imagination. For neither of them would risk it being anything more.

"There you are," Maude exclaimed, smiling at them as she melted out of the crowd. Maude exclaimed, smiling at them. "I must say, you two were *quite* the sight dancing together." She looked back and forth between them knowingly. "People could not take their eyes off of you."

"No doubt," Charles said dryly.

"Of course, there are others who would like a chance to dance with the belle of the ball." Amusement lit Maude's eyes when she looked at Grace. "Or would it be safe to say the belle is already spoken for and wishes to spend time elsewhere?"

"The belle is spoken for." Such an odd thing to say after knowing Charles for so little time. "However, you have gone to such expense, so naturally, I will dance with others if you wish."

"I wish no such thing." Maude beamed at them as though everything had fallen right into place. "The whole point of tonight was to help you find the husband you wanted, sister. Blake and I could not be more pleased that you have chosen Lord Newcastle." She might have left it at that, but she would not be Maude if she did. "Especially after watching you two dance. It was quite clear you are—"

"Looking forward to marrying," Grace interrupted before Maude said something that would, without doubt, make things uncomfortable. "As soon as possible."

"How delightful." Maude's smile grew sunnier still. "We shall post the banns and begin planning the wedding straight away. It shall be a grand affair for one of my favorite sisters."

"Take care, Grace," Abby would say. *"If you do not clarify things, Maude will give you the kind of wedding I prefer. One I highly suspect you and Charles would find equally disagreeable based on his growing unease."*

"I think, perhaps, we would prefer something simpler with very few people." Grace gave him a look that he need not fear. "Is that not right, my lord?"

"That would be preferable," he said without hesitation. "Sooner rather than later, at that."

"I see." Undoubtedly having hoped to throw at least a partially grand wedding, Maude's smile faltered. "How soon, precisely?"

"I would think as soon as we are able." Grace perked her eyebrows at Charles. "Perhaps in a month or so?"

"That quickly?" Maude put a hand to her heart and glanced back and forth between them dubiously. "Are you not worried how scandalous that might seem?"

"Not remotely." Charles looked at Grace in question. "You, my lady?"

"Not at all." Even though she knew Maude cared nothing for scandal and everything about spoiling Grace with a lavish wedding, she played along and squeezed her sister's hand in reassurance. "You need not fret, my dear. Lord Newcastle and I are past the age of worrying about the conclusions some might draw at a hasty marriage. On the contrary, we find we have much in common, and, to our way of thinking, which is more than enough to begin a life together."

"I suppose it must be these days." Maude sighed yet remained hopeful. "But if you change your mind, we can still plan a grand affair. You can take the time to perhaps court and let the mutual affection I just saw—"

"We are decided," she clarified again before Maude continued. As it were, her sister had already said enough to make Grace's cheeks uncomfortably warm. "We will discuss the details with you and Lord MacLauchlin at everyone's convenience."

"If you insist."

"We do."

Maude glanced between them again as though she meant to give it one last try but decided against it and smiled broadly. "Then we shall all have a good chat soon."

Before they could reply, Maude was off, and they were alone once more.

"I think that went relatively well," she said.

"Well enough." Yet hesitation lingered in his eyes. "While I am not looking for a typical marriage, if you wish to have a larger wedding, I would not fault you."

"Do you wish a larger one?"

"Not in the least."

"Then on that, we are in agreement." She considered him as they continued strolling. "If it would not be too much trouble, I would not mind visiting your estate with Alexander while we wait on the banns. It would give him a chance to acclimate before such a big move."

Based on how he tensed, something about that did not sit well, and she called him on it, preferring to keep things straightforward between them. "What is it, my lord? Would you rather I visit alone first?"

"It is not that. Alexander is most welcome." He sipped his whisky and frowned. "My concern lies in the state of my home. Or rather, its current lack of furnishings."

"I am well aware of your lack of furnishings and care not."

He seemed taken aback by that. "And how is it you know such?"

"Because I have made a point of learning more about you." She arched an eyebrow. "Did you not think I would educate myself before proposing to a man? Especially one with whom I would be trusting the care of my son?"

"And what did you discover, my lady?" he said rather tightly.

"That you are a much kinder soul than you let on," she said. "Amongst other things we will discuss in good time."

"Why discuss what you already know?"

"Because I think it would benefit us both," she said. "Perhaps even help us forge a friendship, as that would benefit all parties involved, would it not?"

"Perhaps." He seemed warier than ever. "Though it seems a bit more than we agreed to."

"Oh, I do not know." She was not surprised he fought such a simple thing. "I think you saw a friendship plausible, or you would not have come tonight."

"You are not the most disagreeable person I have ever met," he relented.

"I would hope not." She was about to go on when the last person she expected entered the great hall. Someone she imagined might not be pleased she was marrying for anything but love.

Chapter Six

TO BE EXPECTED, there was a noticeable stir in the crowd when their graces, Lord Jacob and Lady Prudence, the Duke and Duchess of Argyll, were announced. Charles had spent time with Jacob as boys, and though they did not see one another frequently nowadays, he considered him as close a friend as Blake.

"There you are dear sister." Caring little for decorum, Prudence embraced Grace, held her at arm's length, and eyed her affectionately. "You look more beautiful than ever. Truly lovely."

"I had no idea you would be coming tonight." Grace smiled. "Where is my precious little nephew? I cannot wait to see him."

"The nursemaid is putting him to bed, but you two shall reunite first thing tomorrow." Prudence's eyebrows swept up. "Meanwhile, where else would I be on such a night?"

"Hello, old friend." Jacob clasped Charles' shoulder and grinned. "I cannot tell you how good it is to see you here." He introduced him to Prudence. "Newcastle and I go way back. He is a fine chap."

Prudence smiled warmly at Charles. "So nice to meet you, my lord."

The knowing way her gaze flickered from Grace back to Charles told him she was fully aware that Blake and Maude saw them as a match.

He bowed at the waist. "Nice to meet you as well, Your Grace."

"At last," Blake exclaimed, joining them. "All my friends in one place for the first time in ages." He urged them to follow him. "Come, join me in the drawing room for a drink before the masses get hold of you."

"That sounds splendid." Prudence linked arms with Grace. "You must tell me all about this ball of yours, sister." She smiled from Charles to Grace. "For I suspect I have already missed exciting things, indeed."

While Grace seemed happy enough, he caught a flicker of wariness in her eyes that had not been there before. Did she fear what Prudence would think of their agreement? More to the point, would her opinion sway Grace?

He could admit the concept troubled him and not for the reason it should. Rather, he tensed at the thought of Grace backing out of their marriage arrangement and not seeing her again. Because the truth was, however wary it made him, he liked the idea of getting to know her better and becoming friends.

That was it, of course. Nothing more. Or so he tried to convince himself.

He had been stunned by her kiss. Swore he still felt the warmth of her lips on his cheek. If that were not enough, dancing with her had caught him equally off guard. He had been convinced he would only grow more frustrated by all the disagreeable glances, but he was hardly aware of them while he spun Grace on the dance floor.

How could he be, when he became so completely aware of her?

They fit together perfectly as they moved. Too perfectly. He could not remember the last time a woman had felt like that in his arms. The last time he could not look away from her lovely face. If anything, he'd become ensnared by Grace's luminous eyes and a sensation he did not foresee. While he dared not look too closely at it, he did not want it gone from his life. For, if nothing else, it could very well be molded into the start of a great friendship.

Again, it *had* to be friendship and nothing more.

Or so he could only hope, given what she had likely learned about him and his estate. While put off that she had done such, he understood it. Respected her for it, given it had everything to do with her son's welfare. He would have done the same had their positions been reversed.

They chatted and caught up once everybody settled in the drawing room with drinks in hand. Eventually, as direct as Maude had been, Prudence looked from Charles to Grace. "Might I assume you have made your choice then, sister? That you intend to marry Lord Newcastle?"

"I do." As frank with them as she had been with Maude, Grace's gaze swept over everyone. "And while we intend to make a show of it in public for Alexander's sake, you should know it is a marriage of convenience, as neither of us wishes to suffer love again."

"How very—" Prudence seemed to search for the right word—"pragmatic of you." She cocked her head. "Whatever will you do if it becomes more, and you are trapped in the bounds of matrimony, unable to escape?"

"It will not," Charles and Grace said at the same time.

"But if it does?" Prudence mused and sipped from her claret.

"Then we will do our best to steer it back to friendship." Quite confident, Grace offered a firm nod. "Simple as that."

"I should hope not, but of course, that would be up to you." Prudence tilted her head in consideration. "Quite confusing for Alexander, I would think, though. As it were, did you not want to give him the impression that love was part of this union?" The duchess tapped her glass. "I would imagine, knowing my nephew, that true affection between you would be preferable. Furthermore, he might spot something insincere more readily than you may think, as I have heard children are more observant than we credit them."

Prudence made a good point, so Charles felt the same sense of uncertainty that flashed in Grace's eyes. Even so, it was something best left between the two of them to address when alone if need be. Certainly not in front of her sisters and their husbands. To that end, he gave Jacob a look he hoped his friend understood.

Now was not the time for such talk.

"On that, we agree, my dear," Jacob said, clearly taking the hint from Charles. "But I suspect they will figure that out on their own." His friend raised his glass. "To that end, I propose a toast to Lord Newcastle and Lady Howard that their impending marriage, though but an arrangement, be everything they desire."

"Here, here." Blake raised his glass. "To arrangements, and all they might entail."

Prudence raised her glass. "Entail indeed."

Grace's cheeks had pinkened by the time she raised her glass, yet she held her ground. "Here is to arrangements and newborn friendship."

Charles met their toast without adding to it. If anything, he was ready to end this conversation. He had not expected it. Yet he understood now that Blake and Maude wanted this to happen. They saw something he hoped to avoid, yet his mind kept drifting back to the dance floor. To the way Grace had felt in his arms. A sensation he could only hope was fleeting.

The sisters eventually drifted off to find Maude, leaving him alone with Blake and Jacob.

"I fear I must mingle soon, but I thought to purpose something before I did, Charles," Jacob said. "As I am sure you are aware, the MacLauchlins and I, along with the MacLeods, have been resurrecting old buildings throughout Scotland and thought to expand our project to Newcastle. It may not be Scottish, but its history is worth investing in, as are you, my friend."

While he appreciated the offer, he saw things clearly enough, and pride reared its head. Pride he had struggled to push back since this all began.

"Are Grace's sisters growing worried about her ending up with me?" He swirled the whisky in his glass and eyed his friends. Considering how neglectful he had become, her siblings would have every right to feel that way. To want to hover close in case Grace needed them. "Because I assure you, I will take our arrangement most seriously for Alexander's sake, if nothing else."

"We do not doubt you will." Blake sighed. "But if you must know, we are as worried about you as her sisters are of Grace. You have been down an especially difficult road, and she is of a different nature than Maude, Prudence, and Abby. More susceptible to...seeing things one way when they are quite another. More forgiving, by far."

"Some might say seeing things one way rather than another applies to most of us," he said, coming to her defense. "Either way, from what I have seen thus far, she is the very opposite. Rather, she appears to see things more clearly than most." He shrugged a shoulder. "As to being forgiving, is that not a favored trait?"

"It is to a degree," Jacob granted. "But when it is taken advantage of by a supposedly loving husband to the point of gambling away their estate and her dowry until she is left with very little, some might consider it a problem."

"I had not heard that of her late husband." But then, he had cared not for the comings and goings of his society for years. Nor did he care much for gambling.

This explained Blake supplementing her dowry, though.

All aside, he saw what this was really about. "When all is said and done, must Grace be faulted for being too forgiving when she undoubtedly had little say over what her late husband did with their finances?" He downed his whisky and considered his friends. "I see the parallels you are drawing, however. So, should I assume your gestures of extraordinary goodwill are a means for you and your wives to keep an eye on how I handle my affairs once Grace and Alexander are under my roof?"

"You can assume anything you like." Jacob did not mince

words. "But know this. We have worried about you over the years just as much as Grace's sisters have her, and with good reason. That said, yes, we will likely be keeping an eye on you just like you would have us had our situations been reversed. From what I have seen in the short time we have been here, however, I think those days will soon be behind us. That Blake and Maude were right to assume you and Grace would make a good match."

"Arrangement," he corrected.

"Call it what you will," Jacob said. "Whether you like it or not, I see how you look at her, and it does my heart good. Gives me hope where I thought hope might be lost."

Had he been looking at her a certain way? He feared he might have been and would make a point not to, going forward. In the meantime, he would deny such.

"I fear you are mistaken." He set aside his glass and frowned at Blake. "I will say this, though. It makes me uncomfortable marrying her when she does not have all the facts upfront. Why can I not tell her you intend to bring your shipping venture to my port?"

"Because Maude fears Grace's pride would prevent it," he said. "As is, the help we have offered thus far has not been easy for her. Knowing that her selected groom won such a prize on top of that would be offensive on several levels, and be considered one gift too many, I suspect."

"Because God forbid she be considered the prize," he murmured, understanding why she might shun yet another hand-out. Especially one so sizeable.

"Maude asked this of me, so I am asking it of you," Blake went on, refilling Charles' glass. "Tell Grace once you are married if you wish, as she will see us there eventually, but not before. If you do, I fear she will redirect her efforts, and they may not land her in as safe an arrangement as she will have with you."

Or one as easily controlled by her family. "Only ever an arrangement to be sure if I am not honest sooner," he muttered before he could stop himself.

Yet he understood Blake's concern. If she were too prideful to remain under this roof and refused to marry someone who accepted MacLauchlin's business as part of her dowry, there would be others willing to claim her. Those who already had enough money and wanted her only for her title. Her connection to a viscount and duke. That sort would care nothing for her and even less for her son.

And he would not have that.

"Yet an arrangement is all you desire, yes?" Jacob prompted, referring to Charles' quip that if he were not honest with Grace up front, it would eliminate anything more than friendship.

He ignored the comment and thought about it before relenting.

"I will not tell her." He sighed and made things clear. "Until we are married. Then she must know straight away."

"Of course." Blake raised his glass again and smiled. "Then I propose a new toast. To you and Lady Howard enjoying a fine arrangement and a good friendship that benefits all three of you well into the future."

"I second that." Jacob raised his glass as well. "May life bless your upcoming arrangement in unexpected and wondrous ways."

Though he narrowed his eyes at that, he toasted regardless and could admit, however hesitantly, that he felt more hopeful than he had in years. For his community, naturally. Yet deep down, he knew it was more than that. A spark of something other than the gloom he had felt for so long. A sense of anticipation that had everything to do with meeting Grace. Because the truth of the matter? He had grown especially lonely of late and wondered what it might be to hear more than a servant or two shuffling around his estate. Perhaps enjoy lively conversation and company at dinner with a friend.

Something he enjoyed sooner rather than later when he and Grace crossed paths again a short time later. If he was not mistaken, she had been relieved to see him. Not to mention, eager to be free of the would-be suitors swamping her.

"Ah, there you are, darling." Taller than the lot of them, he shouldered past her admirers and held out his elbow. "Might we dine together?"

"Indeed, my lord." Grace flashed him a smile that made it hard to think straight. "I am famished." She slipped her arm through his and bid everyone a good evening before speaking softly enough that they did not overhear. "Many thanks for rescuing me."

"My pleasure." More than she knew. Most certainly more than he would admit. "Are you truly hungry?"

It turned out she was, so they entered the dining room and enjoyed a lovely meal together. Fortunately, she sat to the right of him this time, where he could more easily see her rather than across from him next to besotted hopefuls, and he found it a relief. He enjoyed spending time with her. While he was acutely aware of the dirty looks others had cast before, he did not see them this go around.

Rather, he saw only her as they enjoyed dinner.

Although he was long out of practice at smiling and laughing, he liked watching her do both. Then again, neither was false when it came to Grace. Her laughter was not the grating tinkle made by flirtatious ladies but heartfelt. A pleasant, husky chuckle. Genuine. And her smiles? As if designed to put him at ease, they were soft and encompassing.

"I must apologize," she said after they had finished eating and were strolling through the castle again. "My sisters can come across a bit intensely sometimes, but they meant no harm earlier when we shared our marital plans with them."

"Good, because I was not harmed." And so that she would not fret, he added, "Nor was I offended. It is clear they care about you."

"Do you have siblings?"

"I had an older brother, but he died when I was young," he said. "Fortunately, Lord MacLauchlin and the Duke of Argyll—or the Lord of Rothesay as he was known at the time—felt like brothers, so I did not feel such a deep void, for they filled that space. My family's estate is close enough to the Scottish border that I often saw them often growing up. My parents thought it important I mingle with the Scottish peerage as much as the English."

"I am sorry to hear about your brother but glad you found siblings of a sort with the viscount and duke." She looked at him curiously. "Yet you make it sound like they were more like your brothers back then compared to now."

"Do I?" Thinking of their grand plans regarding him and Grace, he could not help but chuckle. "If anything, they are more my brothers now than ever."

"He laughs." She stopped and smiled with pleasure. "And I cannot help but think it suits you. That you should do it more often."

"Was that a laugh?" He could not remember the last time he had done such. "It felt a tad less robust than that."

"Only because I suspect it is rather foreign sounding to your own ears." Grace's smile softened. Her gaze lingered on his face in a fashion unlike others. They did not look at him, and he'd found that a good thing. He would have shied away for fear of repelling them. Yet Grace did not appear put off. Instead, she seemed comfortable looking at him. Perhaps, however fanciful the notion, even enjoyed such.

"I do so hope we can strive for friendship," she went on. "That you would like it to be part of our arrangement, my lord."

"Charles."

She lifted an eyebrow at him. "Are we at that intimacy already?"

"Given we are marrying soon, I would like to think so." He offered a relenting tilt of his head. "And if we are striving for friendship, of course."

"Of course—" her lovely lips curled up—"Charles." She cocked her head in question. "We were quite defiant to the others in our rush to marry. Did you have another timeline in mind rather than the one I presented?"

"No, I thought to leave that up to you, whether it be a month or longer," he said. "More pointedly, what do you think would work best for Alexander?"

In truth, he hoped she chose straight away. Not because of her dowry or Blake's business but because he wanted her around. He found the idea of returning to the silent seclusion of his mind rather glum. Even so, she must understand that this was up to her. "Might you prefer Alexander to see a slightly longer courtship so that everything is, as you desired, more believable?"

He waited with bated breath and hoped the hesitation on her face meant that he had made a good point.

"I tend to think seeing what we share over the next month will be enough." She thought about it. "A month during which he might see more of you? Not just here but, as aforementioned, at your estate? He has suffered a lot of transition, so visiting where he will live before moving in might be beneficial. Plus, that leaves time for our banns to be contested."

A month when the one behind them had already seemed too long? He might have thought such a relatively short period dreadful before, but now it felt quite the opposite. "I think that sounds more than acceptable, my lady."

She issued a soft smile. "Grace."

"Grace." The name suited her. "A month it is."

And what a month it would be. One that showed him just how clever Blake and Maude had been, after all. Moreover, how clearly they had seen something he had not.

Chapter Seven

"THE NIGHT ENDED that abruptly?" Prudence asked the next day as Grace and her sisters enjoyed tea together. "You and Lord Newcastle decided to marry a month from now, and he decided the evening was over? Then, just like that, he left?"

"Well, it was not *just* like that." She recalled how their eyes had caught when she insisted he called her Grace. How his gaze had drifted to her lips. "There might have been a moment of..." *What, exactly?* Best to proceed carefully with her sisters because the good Lord knew nowadays they were hopeless romantics. "I suppose we shared what some might call a moment of mutual comradery first."

They had just spent a lovely morning with their children before enjoying some much-needed time alone. Alexander was quite fond of Prudence's boy, who was a little angel, to be sure. The perfect mix of his mother and father.

"A moment of *mutual comradery* with Lord Newcastle?" Maude released a dainty snort and smirked. "I know you are determined to remain faithful to William until your dying breath, Grace, but even I would not be such a fool to think mere *comradery* was on either of your minds. Not with a man who looks like that."

"He *is* roguishly handsome." Prudence eyed Grace a little too knowingly as she tittered on to Maude. "You should have heard the gossip surrounding him last night when the wives did not think their husbands were paying them any mind."

"Oh, I did." Maude hid behind her fan and mimicked one. "Dear Heavens, what is Lady Howard thinking dancing with such a brute? Granted, he *is* very masculine, is he not?" Her gaze drifted below Prudence's waist as though looking somewhere quite inappropriate on a man. She rounded her eyes. "Dear me, perhaps a bit *too* masculine."

"My, *my*." Prudence hid behind her fan and rounded her eyes back as if another frivolous woman responded. "You might just be right." She fanned herself. "Just look at those thighs. Those barbaric shoulders. He is most certainly a warrior like all these big burly MacLauchlins glaring down from their age-old portraits." Quite matter-of-fact, she nodded once. "And he has the battle wounds to prove it."

"Who knew the English could make such strapping beasts." Maude fanned herself as well. "Can you imagine him astride a warhorse?" She winked. "Better yet, riding far more enjoyable things."

"They did *not* say that," Grace admonished, caught between a blush and a chuckle.

"That and more." Prudence chuckled as well. "You have been away from all these upper crust wives for some time. Rest assured, the Scots are as direct and risqué as the English regarding men like Lord Newcastle." She rolled her eyes. "Most attractive men, for that matter. He just seems to set their imaginations afire more than most for obvious reasons. And now that you have claimed one another, expect their interest to intensify."

"We have not *claimed* each other," she denied. "We are going into a marital agreement that benefits us mutually."

"I am sure those tittering wives agree completely." Maude put a hand to her heart and grinned from Prudence to Grace. "How could they not after seeing how he looked at you?"

"You mean only had eyes for her." Prudence met Maude's grin. "Both on and off the dance floor, from what I hear."

Had he? Surely not. She sipped her tea rather than show any response other than good reason. "Gossip is not to be trusted."

"Perhaps." The corner of Prudence's mouth inched up. "But my own eyes are, and while I might not have been here for your now-infamous waltzes, I saw clearly the gossip is very accurate this time."

"Indeed." Having sent the servants along so they could chat privately, Maude refreshed their teas. "Whatever your motives going into this marriage of convenience, Grace, I do believe Lord Newcastle is at long last seeing the light of day again." She smiled. "You are that light, of course, and with good reason. You are quite the catch."

"I could not agree more," Prudence echoed. "And whether this is a marriage of convenience or not, his admiration is preferable even if you two decide not to give into love again." She narrowed her eyes. "I see your brow furrowing, Grace, and will not have it. As you surely knew when I arrived, I was going to be a thorn in your side when it came to this because I realize now just how important love is. That said, I will speak my mind and hope, whether you have sworn it off for life or not, that you rediscover such too."

"But you will graciously accept it if I do not," she made clear. "You will accept my wishes and what I want from a marriage to Lord Newcastle, no matter your opinion?"

Prudence hesitated a moment before confirming. "Of course."

"And without constant nudging," she prompted.

"Now that I will not promise." Prudence shrugged and took a dainty sip of tea. "Like Maude, I am your older sister. Therefore, I know best."

Grace looked skyward. "And here I thought you were back to being your less-trying self because of the mad love you found with your husband."

"Oh, darling, this *is* less trying." Prudence grinned and winked. "Anything that helps you find the passion Maude and I have found in our marriages is worth a bit of nagging."

"Rediscovered passion, of course," Maude clarified a little too dutifully to Prudence. "For Grace knows well what it feels like already."

She did. The romance between her and William had been most intense. Quite spectacular when he was home rather than out gambling. He came to her bed often enough, and their lovemaking was fulfilling. Mostly. Usually. As long as she was able to push past her worry over their finances. What their future would look like if they lost everything. What might happen to Alexander. How they would care for him if William's addiction took him one step too far.

She and her sisters went on to talk about other things, but old worries were not far from her mind. What if Charles was no different than William? She understood melancholy and its effects on a person, but what if the negligence of his estate was more than that? If he had a gambling problem like her former husband? One hidden from idle gossip below stairs.

While tempted to set it from her thoughts and continue with Charles without addressing it, she found she could not travel that road again. Refused to. So, when next he arrived at MacLauchlin Castle later that week to escort her back to his estate for a visit, she voiced her concerns as they strolled through the gardens beforehand.

"I fear I rushed into things without having a complete picture, and for that, I apologize." She was even more aware of him than last time, but who could blame her, considering what her sisters had shared? Blast them for no other reason than her traitorous gaze nearly wandered to his reportedly muscular thighs. Worse yet, other things. "More so, I realize now that I should not have held back what I learned about you nor who I learned it from."

"I agree." He urged her to sit beside him on a bench between hedges, giving her the spot that shaded her eyes from the rising sun. "Do go on."

She told him everything she had heard, which had come from

below stairs. Had to, as her thoughts had rarely strayed from him since last they met. Sometimes she worried about him. Other times, she feared him and how quickly she had pulled him into her life. Was she thinking clearly? Was he? Somehow what they intended to do felt rushed yet, at the same time, taking far too long. She felt a strange mix of hesitation and anticipation all at once.

"I understand that gossip is gossip and not always to be trusted, but as you know, I prefer to go into this with honesty." She folded her hands on her lap and hoped she sounded calm despite feeling the opposite. *Had she ever been so nervous? So wary? So hopeful?* "Is it true you let your estate fall into neglect out of grief? That you abandoned your businesses? Sold off your precious family heirlooms to help support your community when you could not be there for them?"

"All but neglecting my businesses is true," he confirmed with nary a hesitation. He seemed to think about it a moment before he shook his head. "No, neglecting my businesses is true, too. For trusting those I did to keep them afloat was neglect in itself. Because rest assured, I would not have let things go as they did if I had been there. Had I overseen things as I should have."

"Were you gambling, then?" she said tentatively, afraid to hear the answer.

Charles' eyebrows lowered sharply. "Gambling? Never. I tried it once and loathed it." He shook his head. "Unluckiest chap you will ever meet." He shrugged one broad shoulder, drawing her eye to the way it strained against his overcoat. "Honestly, I was just blinded by misery and self-loathing. And whilst we agreed not to use the word anymore, above all, pity. Bitterness. Hatred at the world for taking my wife and unborn child. At the war for taking...what it took."

"And what was that?" she asked softly, curious how he saw things. Where she thought he would say his eye or mention his blemished features, he surprised her.

"It took my youth," he said. "My confidence and carefree

nature." His voice dropped an octave. "Worst of all, though, it took my faith in mankind. My *love* for mankind."

Understandable. Every last bit. She knew little of fighting in a war and suffering such injuries, but she valued her liberties. Those who had fought for them. *What to say to him, though? How to relate without sounding disingenuous? Simply, she supposed.*

As she saw him here and now.

"You might feel like you lost your youth, but I still see a young man." And she did. A distractingly attractive one at that. His top hat shaded most of his face, but sunlight still made clear just how stunning a color his remaining light blue eye was. Outside of his scar, his skin was unscathed. "As to your confidence, you have struck me as more able and unaffected than you think. Yet, I cannot speak to a carefree nature as that, too, has been taken from me." She touched his cheek before she could stop herself. "As to faith and love in mankind, I suspect, as much as it feels like it, you have not lost such yet. Rather, you merely await the opportunity to rediscover it."

Had she sounded too bold? So forward? Would he take it as she meant it? Because it could be easily misconstrued, considering her hand lingered on his cheek before she pulled it back and tucked it on her lap again. Still feeling his warmth and faint stubble, she closed her fist and held onto the sensation when she should surely let it go.

His gaze lingered on her face as though he were unsure how to respond before he finally cleared his throat and found his tongue. "We agreed to no longer use certain words, so you make my response limited, other than to say I appreciate your vote of confidence…more than you know. May you be right on all counts."

"I am quite sure I am and will be." She smiled, praying he was just as truthful. "As honest as you were when you denied any possible gambling addiction."

"Honest, to be sure." He considered her. "Might you share why you worry so?"

As if he did not already know. If Maude and Blake were not matchmakers enough, it seemed Prudence and Jacob had also joined in. "If you tell me why you have decided to suddenly steer clear of being truthful with me? Because I am quite sure you are as educated about my past as I am about yours."

He was about to respond when Maude appeared around the corner and outshone the sun. No surprise, given she had found them alone in such a secluded spot. "There you two are."

"Indeed."

When Maude simply looked back and forth between them with approval, Grace prompted her to go on. "What brings you this way, sister?"

"Oh, yes, that." Maude gestured back the way she had come. "Alexander is ready to go." She nodded once. "I even saw overnight clothing packed because a storm brews, and returning this evening might prove difficult."

Grace glanced at the cloud-free morning sky and frowned. "But it is beautiful out."

"Aye," her sister replied, speaking like the Scots she had come to love. "However, the locals claim it will be quite something when it arrives, which will likely be sooner rather than later, so best you set out soon."

When Grace looked at Charles in question, he shrugged and agreed. "I have often been amazed at how well those in these parts can forecast the weather."

"I see." She did, too, because the weather could be just as finicky in her neck of the woods. "Then it seems we best be on our way."

"Are you sure you do not mind Mrs. Catlin and Mr. Hew traveling with us this first time?" she asked yet again as they trailed behind Maude, who seemed to flee rather quickly. No doubt, a means to give them as much time alone as possible. "I fear Alexander has grown accustomed to having them both along. They are rather far from their Wales, too, so I appreciate you allowing them to visit their new home beforehand."

"As I assured you, they are most welcome." He gave her a pointed look as they strolled arm-in-arm. "Because, as I warned, it might be best they understand things up front."

"You *did* say that." Yet he had been rather vague about his meaning. "Is it that bad?" They might have talked about his neglected estate and lack of furnishings, but she had trouble envisioning it. "Surely, it is livable?"

"Livable? Yes." He seemed unsure how to go on. "I would recommend we work toward making it more livable before you and yours move in, though. For your comfort, of course."

"Of course." Sensing he skirted around things as readily as Maude, she slid him a look. Fished for lack of a better word about how bad things really were. *Were there beds? A dining table? Wood on the hearths? Enough food in the pantry?* "As comfort is rather important when one wants a good night's rest. Even better when one desires warmth over chill. Cooked food over raw."

"Some foods are not so bad raw," he reminded. "Vegetables. Certain types of fish. Not meats, I grant you." He slid her one of those rare smiles that made her breath catch. "We have evolved that far…at least beyond my estate."

She met his smile and teased him right back. "So, you and yours have not discovered fire yet?"

"We thought we had, once upon a time." He winked. "Then future generations lost the knowledge."

"Ah." She chuckled. "It does pay to keep records, does it not? For our descendants and the advancement of mankind, naturally."

"Naturally." His humor faded as swiftly as it had arisen. "Joking aside, you must be forewarned that it might not be the most comfortable stay if you are forced to spend the night."

"We will worry about that if and when the time comes." Grace felt rather optimistic regardless. "Who knows? Perhaps it will be an opportunity to assess beginning anew." She realized how that might have sounded after the words escaped her lips. "Apologies, Charles. I did not mean to say that your home will be anything less than welcoming, nor that you need to start anew with me, even if we are married. Ours is no such arrangement."

"No need to apologize," he said softly, "as, one way or another, I will be starting anew with you. For we intend to commit to one another, whether love is involved or not."

"Indeed." And she appreciated him acknowledging it. Understanding that whether they be friends, lovers, or nothing at all, they were about to embark on a longstanding relationship that would keep them in close quarters. That said, respect and concern for each other, as well as unhindered communication, would be most welcome.

"So, you understand you may find my estate rather shocking," he said, reiterating their viewpoints. "And I understand that you always prefer my honesty about such things up front."

"Yes, to both." She found it difficult to stop smiling and had no idea why, other than speaking with him, *being* with him, seemed to breathe much-needed life back into her. Life that, oddly enough, she had no idea she had existed without. "Yet still, I and mine will champion forth to our new home even if we find ourselves quite taken aback."

"Plan on it." He winced and gave her a look. "Moreover, consider yourself warned but know that better days lie ahead."

Somehow, she did not doubt that. Or perhaps that was her inner hope shining through once more. An endless reserve of false optimism built up during the years she'd spent with William.

As it happened, the commute southeast toward Charles' estate on the North Sea was rather pleasant. She sat beside him, and Alexander sat between Catlin and Hew across from them. Her servants were predictably quiet, as was her son. Rather, he eyed Charles when he thought he was not looking. Not glances of repulsion or fear but curiosity.

She had spoken with Alexander about what she intended to do, what *they* would be doing, and why. Most mothers in her situation would not, but she wanted him to understand. To realize they could not remain at MacLauchlin Castle forever.

"So, you are not happy here, Mother?" he had wondered.

"I am very happy, but it cannot be my home always." She had crouched and cupped his cheek. Made sure he understood he would very much be part of this. He was more important than anything. "It cannot be our home." She had pondered the best way to make him understand and decided direct was best. The truth. As much as his young mind could handle, of course. "When Auntie Maude married Uncle Blake, MacLauchlin Castle became her home, their home, so we must do the samc. I must find us a proper home."

"And that will be with Lord Newcastle rather than back at Father's home?"

"It will." She bit back tears at the confusion in his eyes. "Because Father's home is not ours anymore. Instead, Lord Newcastle would like us to share his home with me as his wife. His estate is not all that far from MacLauchlin Castle, so we will be able to visit often enough."

"So, Lord Newcastle is to be my new father?"

While tempted to deny it as he only had one father, she knew it would only confuse him further. By law, Charles would take on guardianship of him and care for him. That had been his promise. Part of their agreement. And she could only pray he honored his word. That she had not been wrong about him.

"Yes, Lord Newcastle will be your new father." She had cupped his other cheek. "But your real father will always remain in our hearts. Lord Newcastle understands that and intends to honor it." She'd shaken her head. "Otherwise, I would not have agreed to marry him."

Alexander had thought about that for a moment. "Then you do not love him like you did Father?"

"No, but I care for him in a loving way." She had continued offering him words of reassurance. "Not just that, but I admire him greatly and think he will offer us a good life. That there is a new adventure to be found with him."

"Is he a pirate then?" He had cocked his head, curious. "Because I have heard the children here at MacLauchlin Castle claim he is. That he fought great battles and would someday steal all the loot from Lord MacLauchlin's Castle with his ruthless ways if it were not well defended."

"I think you know better than that." She had smiled. "Lord Newcastle will never take this fortress because he is no pirate. Rather he was an honorable captain in the Royal Navy. A warrior who has fought to keep all of us safe. Perhaps someday, he will share his war stories with us. But, until then, might we not trust him?" She'd winked. "If nothing else, he is bound to be quite interesting, is he not?"

"It seems so." Alexander had considered her in that wise way he'd developed after his father's death and thought about it a moment before he nodded. "Of course, Mother. If this is what you think is best."

While that had not been not quite the answer she had hoped for, she could not blame him. What else was he supposed to say? Even so, she knew this was the right course of action. *Charles* was the best path for them.

Now she could only pray she was right.

Thus far, the journey had been pleasant, and she imagined one way or another, it always would be with him. Despite some noticeable aging, his carriage could be worse off, which made her optimistic that perhaps he'd exaggerated the condition of his estate. As it were, if his carriage was serviceable, then his home could not be all that bad, right?

"As forecasted." Charles sighed and eyed the sky when thunder rumbled, and it began raining. "The Scots were spot-on."

"So it seems." She wondered at the sudden unease on his face. Was he dreading having them stay the night? "Yet let that not ruin our day."

"One can only hope." He shot them what appeared a resolved look. "Please accept my apologies for the inconvenience."

What did he mean by that? They were not inconvenienced, and she said so before, moments later, she realized what he had been alluding to.

Chapter Eight

OF ALL THE blasted luck. Could the rain not have held off until they arrived at his estate? Naturally not, and as predicted, two drips began toward the center of his carriage.

"Again, apologies." Embarrassed, Charles whipped off his top hat and caught the drops the best he could lest they upset anyone. "I fear my carriage is in need of some repairs."

"No need to apologize, my lord." Grace smiled kindly. "And no need to get your hat wet." She glanced from the other three to him. "A little moisture is not going to harm any of us."

"I quite agree," Mrs. Catlin said, smiling just as kindly.

Might it be but a little moisture, he prayed when an awkward silence fell, broken only by the sound of drops landing in his hat. He could just imagine what her servants thought about their mistress' future with him and what Alexander might be thinking. The boy had been painfully quiet thus far. He glanced at Charles nervously every so often, but mostly he stared out the window.

Until now, that is.

Now he seemed caught unaware by Charles' actions. Or perhaps taken aback that an earl's carriage leaked. He found the child's expression hard to read while he watched Charles try to catch drops.

"We are not too far from my estate," he assured them, cursing under his breath when another drop started right over

Alexander's lap.

Determined to keep the boy dry, he leaned across to catch the next one, but Alexander removed his hat first and caught it.

"I have got this one, Lord Newcastle." Though he spoke quite studiously, the hint of a grin hovered on his face. "Perhaps it best you focus on the others?"

Without doubt, because the rain only fell harder.

"Indeed." He nodded thanks and redirected his hat, only for another and another to start dripping.

"I have this one." Mr. Hew caught the fourth with his hat.

Mrs. Catlin grinned and caught the fifth with her bonnet. "And I, this one."

"Well then, I best get this one." Having already untied her bonnet, Grace grinned and caught the newborn sixth drop. Her eyes were merry rather than dismayed when they turned his way. "Given it was raining the first night we met, I am rather shocked you were not soaked upon arrival, as one hat would have failed indeed."

Thankful for genuine humor rather than mocking levity, he managed to meet her grin. When she laughed, the others did as well and attempted to catch more drops. Even Alexander joined in the fun, laughing as he steered his hat this way and that. Charles could tell by the surprise and pleasure in Grace's eyes that humor was something he rarely indulged in nowadays.

Grace winked at her son and kept chuckling. "Did I not tell you we were on another grand adventure, Alexander?"

"You did, Mother." The boy glanced Charles' way tentatively before his focus returned to the drops, and he spoke softly yet loud enough to hear. "You failed to mention just how fun it would be, though."

Fun? A carriage full of leaks? But he supposed it was as they laughed, and staying dry became quite the game. Something they mostly accomplished before the rain finally turned to a drizzle, and his estate appeared in the distance.

"Oh, my," Grace exclaimed when she spied it. "Is

that…yours?"

"It is." He had been in such a stupor for so long that he hardly took the time to see what others might. Perhaps took his stately castle on a cliff overlooking the sea for granted. But then, it had lost its appeal years ago with the loss of his wife and child. Lost its luster when it stopped being a home and became a prison.

"Wow," Alexander whispered, wide-eyed at the imposing structure.

"Wow, to be sure." Grace looked from the turrets and battlements of his estate to him. "It is breathtaking, my lord. Is it older than MacLauchlin Castle?"

"Yes," he said, "but only by fifty years or so."

"Now, if I am correct, Alnwick Castle is a bit north of here, yes?" Mr. Hew said. "And Edinburgh Castle north of that?"

"That is right." The carriage made its way up the winding drive surrounded by windswept moors. "We passed just north of Newcastle to get here."

"Quite right." Mr. Hew pushed his spectacles up his nose and nodded. "It will be a wonderfully historical area for young Alexander to enjoy."

"Yes, it will." Unlike MacLauchlin Castle, they had done away with the drawbridge and portcullis some time ago. Instead, they passed through gates that led to a circular driveway in front of his estate. "After refreshments, I shall have to give you a tour."

Even though he cringed at the thought, it would be worth it if it kept Alexander smiling. There was no avoiding things now, anyway. They were here, and this would be their new home. So, he set aside his embarrassment as best he could and focused on showing them to the door. He had sold off one of his last precious family heirlooms and hired more staff to start cleaning. A monumental task but the entranceway and great hall were, at last, showing signs of improvement when the door opened, and they entered.

He introduced them to his butler, Mr. Thomas, who nowadays also served as his part-time valet, then to his head housekeeper, Mrs. Bessie. Both had been with him for years, and he could not value them more.

"How beautiful," Grace marveled, eyeing the great hall with the same wonder the others did. She took in the vaulted ceiling and sizeable fireplace with its delicately carved mantle. Again, he tried to see things through their eyes and appreciate the untouchable workmanship of the balustrade and sweeping stairs leading to the floors above. The various arched medieval hallways that branched off in various directions.

He had moved what scant tapestries he had left into a few select rooms, including this one, so at least it did not echo as much as it had before. Fortunately, the fire crackling invitingly in the great hall had helped warm things, as did the one in the drawing room.

Bubbly by nature, Mrs. Bessie smiled warmly at them before she wondered if she might bring Mrs. Catlin and Mr. Hew below stairs to meet the staff.

The way Grace looked to her servants first to make sure that suited them told him the relationship they shared was as unconventional as the one he shared with his servants.

"That would be lovely, Mrs. Bessie." Grace smiled at his housemaid. "Thank you."

"Please see that they receive tea and something to eat," he said to Bessie. "Then perhaps a tour of the castle?"

"Of course, my lord."

"Excellent." Charles urged everyone to hand over their hats to his butler. "Meanwhile, Mr. Thomas will see our hats dried in front of the fire." He grinned at his man. "You may want to focus primarily on the insides versus the outsides."

Although Thomas' eyebrows edged up, either because of the request or a jovialness he was unaccustomed to with his master, he nodded and took the hats. "As you wish, my lord."

Once Bessie left with the other two, he retired to the drawing room with Grace and Alexander to enjoy a spot of tea and some scones. It was strange having visitors in his home but not disagreeable. Although Alexander had grown quiet again, he did not seem as withdrawn as before. Rather, he appeared focused on taking everything in, from the stately windows to the various nooks that made this castle so interesting.

"There is much to see in this castle that one can view quite easily," he said once they resumed their tour. "And much one cannot see because it is hidden."

When Grace told him she would like to bring Alexander here before they married, he worried about how to go about this tour and show a young boy his home. Ultimately, he had decided to do it the way he'd once envisioned showing his son or daughter around once they were old enough to appreciate it.

"Why is much hidden?" Grace asked when it was clear Alexander wanted to but still hesitated to speak freely.

"Because my ancestors needed places to hide during wartime." He led them down a hallway off the drawing room. "Not just that but ways to escape if need be."

"Ah, because this castle sits relatively close to the Scottish border," she deduced.

"Indeed," he said. "As I am sure you know, Edinburgh Castle has changed hands between the English and Scots a great many times over the centuries."

"Which means when the Scots held the castle," Alexander said, as though he could not keep quiet any longer, "the English were more susceptible to raids and whatnot."

"Correct." Pleased that the boy had spoken up, he nodded with approval as they started up a narrow set of winding stairs. "So, it was crucial we English be prepared. More importantly, that our castles could protect our families during times of unrest." He led them into a circular room at the top of one of the north-facing towers and pointed out the various windows. Specifically, the narrower ones. "So, like MacLauchlin Castle, even though we have since installed larger windows, you will still find many arrow-slit windows in most of the higher rooms. Especially the towers."

"Even the sea-facing side?"

"Most especially, the sea-facing ones as ships were just as much a threat, whether French, Scottish, Spanish, or otherwise. Of course, older castles took Vikings into account as well."

"I imagine they did." Alexander narrowed an eye out one of the skinny windows. "Shooting an arrow from here must have been quite difficult."

"Not for a well-trained archer," he said. "And remember, these windows were just as much for protection. As were the battlements." He perked a brow. "Would you like to go up on the one that overlooks the sea?"

He had done his research, so he knew the boy had an affinity for the ocean.

"I would very much like that, my lord." Trepidation swiftly replaced hope when Alexander looked at Grace. "Might I, Mother? Or would you rather I not until I become more accustomed to the area?"

"I suspect if you were going to react to whatever might be in the air here, you would have done so by now, love, so, of course, we can go look at the battlements." She gestured at the satchel Charles had wondered at her carrying. "Mrs. Catlin saw coffee packed, so we are prepared just in case."

What a thing for a boy to worry about, but he could only be glad Grace was ready for any problems that might arise. He had also researched hay fever, so he understood coffee could help open airways. It did not seem like a sound science, but at least it was something. He had no experience dealing with what Alexander suffered but had taken every precaution when it came to what he thought might comfort him.

"Come then." He eyed the darkening sky and urged them to follow him back downstairs. "However temporarily, the rain has let up, so let us retrieve our coats and make our way to the battlement overlooking the water."

"Might we see the hidden rooms afterward, my lord?" Alexander wondered.

Until he better understood the flash of concern in Grace's eyes at that, he opted to keep things mysterious. Besides, it would give the boy something to look forward to as he embarked on a new life here.

"As I am sure you understand, Alexander, they are top secret." Charles gave him a pointed look. "That said, I think it best to wait until you move in and call this castle your own. Become its young master, second only to me. Then you shall learn all its secrets."

Alexander's gaze flashed with excitement before he grew most serious about his upcoming role. "I understand and look forward to learning everything."

Charles nodded in approval before he shot Grace a look of reassurance the moment Alexander became distracted exploring this or that. She, in turn, looked at him with relief and mouthed, *thank you*. A vote of confidence in all this, as he imagined she had noticed how scarce the walls and furnishings were despite being forewarned. How ceilings in some rooms had water stains, and the bricks on many hearths were crumbling.

Fortunately, Alexander seemed oblivious to anything but the structure of the building. Not just its history but its various designs. To the point, he wondered if the boy's future did not lie in architecture. He would have to ask Grace about it. Find out if that was a direction in which to steer his schooling as time passed.

Odd to contemplate such things when a month ago, educating a child living under his roof would have seemed unimaginable. Merely part of a potential past lost to him forever. Yet now, he looked forward to it and felt a growing sense of excitement at what the future might hold. He and Grace may have been determined to remain friends, but that did not mean he could not be a father figure to Alexander. Not to replace but perhaps to fill in the gap left by his lost father.

He hoped Grace would open up to him about her challenges with her late husband's gambling addiction. How or if it had affected Alexander. He could only imagine what life must have been like for her. While she had loved William, what a difficult thing to live with, especially when dealing with an ailing child who needed the financial security only his father could provide.

"Here we are," he said once they reached the door leading out to the battlement. He made things clear to Alexander. "The wind will be especially biting, so keep your coat buttoned to the top and hold tight to the winter cap Mr. Thomas gave you."

Alexander held his hat down on either side of his face just to be safe and nodded. "Yes, my lord."

"Very good." He opened the door and sheltered Grace against the brunt of the salty wind as they made their way along the wall walk. White-tipped frothing waves crashed against unforgiving rock below, and seagulls cried overhead. "The fog grows especially thick here, so a lighthouse is just there." He pointed at a faint, flickering light in the distance. "Built nearly a hundred years ago, it has saved many a ship from losing its way and crashing against these cliffs."

"Have you traveled to it?" Alexander's eyes grew more curious still. "If so, what was it like?"

"I have, and it is quite impressive." He smiled. "If you would like, and do not fear sailing, I will take you there someday."

Despite how unsavory the idea of being on the open sea again, he would push past it if it meant getting his businesses back in good standing. Push past it for the sake of Grace and Alexander and the financial security he was determined to provide them.

"I do not fear it at all." Alexander's gaze grew wondrous as he looked from Charles to the lighthouse. "So, I would very much like to go there, my lord."

Charles could not help but smile. "Then we shall do it to be sure."

"Thank you," Grace said softly when, with her permission, Alexander set to exploring the battlement and admiring the sea. "You are being very gracious to him, and I appreciate it more than you know."

"No need to thank me." He continued angling his body to

take the gusty wind's brunt. It had such a bite he wondered if they might see a touch of ice and snow with the incoming storm because the bulk of bad weather had clearly not arrived yet. "He is a fine boy, Grace."

"He is." A nostalgic smile curved her mouth as she watched Alexander. "I have not seen him this happy in a long time."

Based on how she said it, he could not help but wonder if that happiness had started fading even before his father passed.

"Well, I hope he continues to find happiness here." While tempted to pull her close when she shivered, he dared not. Instead, he wrapped his coat around her shoulders. "Tell me, why the hesitation about bringing him into the hidden rooms and hallways?"

She frowned. "Are you not cold without a jacket?"

"Not in the least." He had braved weather far colder during wartime.

Clearly unconvinced, Grace eyed him for a moment before she went on. "I am concerned about Alexander being in the hidden areas of your castle because I suspect them quite stale and dusty." She worried at her lower lip when she glanced at Alexander. "Areas like that could very well set off his hay fever."

"Understandable." He cringed at the overall state of his castle. "Perhaps I should see more windows opened for a time, in general? Despite the slow resurrection of things, I imagine there is still much dust about."

"Your castle is lovely and coming along beautifully," she praised. "No need to open windows. As you heard me tell Alexander downstairs, if he was going to react adversely to it or our surroundings, I believe he would have by now." She sighed. "You see, different areas invoke different responses."

"That makes sense as different things grow in different areas," he said. "Leaving the dust varied, I would imagine."

"Exactly right."

"Even so," he said, "might we consider a covering of some sort over his mouth and nose when we finally explore the hidden areas here? Such helped during battle when smoke grew cloying, so it stands to reason it might do the same for dust."

"I think that a clever idea." Gratefulness lit her eyes when she looked at him. "I believe more by the moment that I made a very wise decision proposing to you."

He found it amusing that she viewed it that way, for he swore it was the other way around. Either way, he agreed and said as much.

"I must apologize once again for my lack of furnishings," he said, needing to point out the obvious for his own sanity. To have things out in the open rather than quietly assessed. "I have hired more staff and intend to begin refurnishing with time, starting with tapestries as they do help hold in the warmth." He hesitated a moment but figured if they were to be friends and share a life here, she deserved to have a say. "I thought perhaps as we spend time together over the next month, you might like to help me choose things to your taste? I know you will come with belongings of your own, but still. I want you to feel comfortable here. Part of this place."

"How very changed you are from the man who sat next to me at MacLauchlin Castle not all that long ago," she said softly. "Yet I admit to suspecting a different version of you dwelled within all along."

Her eyes grew rather tender as her gaze lingered on his face in that special way of hers. In a fashion that dissuaded him from shying away in shame but instead made him want to return her affectionate regard.

"I appreciate and accept your offer to purchase furnishings together, Charles," she continued. "But only under one condition."

Anything. "And that is?"

"That we choose things to your taste as well." Her voice dropped an octave. "They might not be able to replace your family heirlooms, but they should still have the power to invoke fond sentiments years from now."

Something about the way she said that gave him pause. Almost as if she presented the idea that such sentiment would come solely from the two of them purchasing future items together. As if, perhaps, he would look back on them as those lovely but foolish days when they thought mere friendship would be enough.

"Condition accepted," he said gruffly, unable to drag his gaze from her stunning face. Unable to focus on anything but her, for that matter. The rosy glow of her cheeks from the chilly air. The way she tended to worry at her plush lower lip, drawing his eyes there only for his imagination to again wander into uncharted territory. Or should he say territory he thought never to revisit? Yet visit his stubborn thoughts did, as he wondered what her lips might feel like beneath his. What it would be like to kiss a woman again.

This woman.

Her.

How she might taste.

Yet, despite his errant fantasy, he knew better and dragged his gaze away. If he kissed her, it would only complicate things for them both. Make what they intended far more difficult. Because after all was said and done, they were only human and had needs.

Needs he suspected had not been fulfilled for either of them in far too long.

In truth, he had not thought considering matters of the flesh would be necessary with their arrangement as he had not desired a woman since his late wife. Nor would he put one through lying with him in his current state. A state and appearance that clearly did not affect Grace as it did others. Rather, the way she looked at him made him feel somewhat normal again.

Attractive, even, if such were possible.

"Come." He urged Alexander to join them when lightning flashed over the sea and rain spit again. "The storm will be here soon, and there is plenty more to see inside."

Grace smiled when Alexander's eyes lit with anticipation. An excitement he hoped would carry over to what he wanted to show the boy next. Something he prayed would make him feel welcome. That in mind, he led them to a candlelit hallway that ran along the seaside of the castle until they came to a door halfway down.

"I hope you do not think me too forward, Alexander, but when I knew you would be coming to live here, I wanted to make your stay as comfortable as possible." He opened the door. "Therefore, I hope your new bedroom suits you."

Where he had expected one response, he got quite another.

And it was not from Alexander but Grace.

Chapter Nine

GRACE TRIED NOT to, but when Charles opened the door to the bedroom he had created for Alexander, tears welled. What had he *done*? How could he be so utterly thoughtful? Because he had obviously learned enough about her son to create such. More than that, she suspected, based on its ample content, that he had started with this room when it came to refurnishing.

"Are you all right, Grace?" Charles asked softly as Alexander's eyes rounded in astonishment, and he entered the room. "Is this too much?"

Given he had to have put what finances he could manage toward this room before all others, most definitely, yes, but she could not fault him. Not when a wide smile blossomed on Alexander's face as he took everything in. His wondrous gaze traveled from the tapestries with their stunning seascapes and mighty ships to actual models of equally impressive ships and then to the proud horses on shelves high enough that the figurines could be better admired. There was even an age-old castle or two.

The room had been decorated perfectly for a boy on the verge of manhood, in varying shades of Alexander's favorite color, blue. Boxes of models yet to be put together lay organized on other shelves, waiting for her son, as that was one of his favored past times. His furniture was elegant and masculine but, at the same time, suitable for his age. Everything about this space spoke to Alexander so much she could not help but think Charles knew her son better than his actual father.

Or, at the very least, he had taken the time to educate himself.

"How did you know what..." she began, then trailed off when she figured it out. "Maude told you."

Of course, her sister did. If she thought they were a match, she would do anything to make Charles more appealing in Grace's eyes.

"After I approached her about it," Charles said, "yes, Maude was very helpful. I even spoke with Mrs. Catlin and Mr. Hew, so I might get things just right."

He had done what?

"Truly?" she whispered because she could not quite find her voice. "This was all you?" She wiped away a tear, took it all in, and looked at him again. Tried to understand how one could be capable of such kindness when he had been so bitter and angry not all that long ago. Of which he had every right to be, in her opinion. "You cared that much?"

"Of course." Charles seemed both unsettled and confused by her response. "I hope I did not overstep any boundaries."

"Yet you did." She wiped away another tear as Alexander exclaimed in delight when he realized his room possessed several windows overlooking the sea. While tempted to hold back, she imagined it was too late. And they *had* promised one another honesty. "Though I fear you might misunderstand what kind of boundary you just pushed past, Charles."

She was not surprised to see the confusion on his face as his gaze lingered on her. Enough confusion that she said something she probably should not. Something she somewhat regretted the moment it left her mouth, but her emotions were running high, and her thinking skewed.

Or so she tried to convince herself when she knew her thinking was not off in the least.

"As much as it pains me to remind you, as I am certain you felt such early on, you may want to reflect on how strongly you felt for your unborn child," she said softly enough that they would not be overheard. She swallowed hard and continued. Hoped he understood. "How you might have felt had he been Alexander and someone you were determined to remain friends with showed such incredible kindness? How that might affect so very much?"

His confusion lingered a moment longer before his pupils flared, and he seemed to understand her meaning. Understood that the way to a mother's heart, however unavailable and broken she thought it, was through her child. More pointedly, he tested a heart that might be alive and well after all.

One, more dauntingly still, ready to be pieced back together.

Noticeably uncomfortable, he cleared his throat and made to respond but became distracted by Alexander when he stopped in front of Charles, bowed from the waist, and handled all of this quite properly. "My deepest thanks for your hospitality, Lord Newcastle. I quite like this room." His stern expression gave way to a barely-repressed smile. "Quite a bit, indeed."

"I could not be happier to hear that, Master Alexander." He met her son's smile. "In time, I look forward to building a model or two with you if you would like the assistance?"

Quickly tempered delight flashed in Alexander's eyes. "I very much would, my lord."

"Charles," he corrected, seeming to throw caution to the wind when it came to her warning. "When we are alone or with family, I insist you call me by my given name."

When Alexander looked at her in question, more so for her permission as well, she nodded that he should do as Charles asked.

Alexander's small smile never wavered when his attention returned to Charles. "Very well then, Captain Charles."

Although surprise flashed in Charles' eyes that Alexander knew he had been a captain, he did not speak to it. Rather, despite appearing fine enough with her son calling him such, it seemed a title unworthy of acknowledging.

"So, what do you think, young Alexander?" Mrs. Bessie asked, appearing in the doorway. She rested a hand against her ample bosom and smiled broadly as though she had never been so delighted to see anyone. "Shall we begin working on one of those models now and get to know one another better while your good ma and Lord Newcastle spend some time together?"

Grace could not help but think her timing rather opportune. Perhaps intentional.

Alexander gave Grace a hopeful look. "Might I, Mother?"

"Absolutely." She smiled kindly at Charles' maid, who she suspected was as close to him as Catlin was to Grace. "Thank you, Mrs. Bessie."

Bessie's cherub cheeks blossomed pink, and she curtsied. "Of course, my lady." She beamed at Alexander. "We shall enjoy ourselves *immensely*."

Convinced they would, Grace smiled at her son and followed Charles back into the hallway, quick to apologize once they were alone. "I am sorry for what I said before." She shook her head and looked at him rather than shy away, so he saw the regret in her eyes. "It was highly inappropriate of me to mention your child like that. To draw such a comparison."

"I agree." Charles urged her to walk with him and veered down another hallway. "Yet I also disagree because I want you to feel you can be honest with me always. Even if it means bringing up painful subjects." He opened another door and led her into a bedroom with nothing but a cradle resting in the corner. "To that end, I feel you should see this." He gestured at said cradle. "To understand it is the only thing remaining of what was originally in this room because Mrs. Bessie and Mr. Thomas convinced me to keep it. Servants who have been with me since I was a boy."

"This would have been his or her nursery?" she said softly, understanding. "And that, his cradle?"

"Yes," he confirmed. "It is one of the few family heirlooms I have yet to sell." His troubled gaze swept around the room. "All the others that made up this nursery are gone." He sighed. "Auctioned away with much anger in my heart, I am afraid."

"I can well understand, but I admit to being glad the cradle is still here." More so, that he had let her in enough to share such with her. To let her know that a piece of what he had lost still remained. So perhaps it had not been so terribly offensive to mention his child. Even so. She steered clear of using their dreaded words, sympathy or empathy. Especially right now. "Again, I am so very sorry for having brought up—"

"No." He shook his head. "If we are to be frank with one another, then it must cover all things. Apply to not just the past but the present and future."

She stilled when he came close and looked at her in a way that made her breath catch. Made her knees grow weak and reasonable thought impossible.

"That said, Lady Howard…" His voice grew hoarse, and he clenched his fist as though he fought to keep from touching her. "I fear we might have underestimated our marital arrangement. Underestimated to what level we truly wish to remain married to our pasts."

Heat rushed through her at the desire in his eyes. At the way his gaze fell to her lips and lingered as though it were taking everything in him not to kiss her. His breathing quickened along with hers when he shifted a fraction closer. Yet again, she felt that same heightened sense of awareness she had experienced when waltzing with him, and their bodies had been so close.

"I…" She shook her head. "We…" *What was she trying to say?* She had never felt so much fear and anticipation at once. *Was she betraying William, or would he want this? Be happy for her? How could he be when she meant to…wanted to…* "I cannot."

"Nor I," Charles whispered. His gaze lingered on her face in tortured silence before he stepped away.

Not before she caught his hand, though. "Yet might we consider—"

"We might." Before she knew what hit her, he pulled her against him and cupped her cheek. "Not here. Not now. But you might revise the stipulation of our arrangement if you wish." Where she thought for sure he would kiss her this time, he instead rested his forehead against hers and released a choppy breath it seemed he had been holding for a lifetime. "Because I wish...*hope* now, where I thought hope lost."

She closed her eyes and rested her hand on his warm chest. Struggled to catch her breath and hear past the slam of her heart as she encountered the power of his heartbeat beneath her palm. Tried to comprehend anything beyond him and how his presence consumed her senses, from his heat beneath her fingertips to the tremble of his strong body.

He fought this every bit as much but knew it was a losing battle.

"Then we shall revisit..." she managed, her voice strained. While her body wanted one thing, her mind was coherent enough to fight her urges. Her heart? Impossible to know. It felt torn and unsteady. "Revisit the rules of our arrangement after we are married."

"I think that might be best." He pulled back yet continued cupping her cheek. Still looked at her as though it took everything in him not to close his mouth over hers. "While I cannot promise you love, I find I would like—" he paused as though that were not quite the right word—"no, *need*, to hold you. Find comfort in one another's arms that mere friendship will not afford us."

While some might take his declaration as most inappropriate, she understood. She had thought desire and passion lost to her past, but it seemed not. Instead, she felt rather eager.

Suddenly most desperate for her wedding day.

"I am in full agreement." She tilted her cheek into his touch. "Full agreement, indeed." Needing more between now and then, she clutched his shirt, wanting to keep him close. "That said, I would prefer our courting in the meantime to be most genuine." She put a finger to his lips when he issued a slow, knowing smile.

"Not with a stolen kiss or two but with a more genuine affection, I suppose."

"Is that not what we have already been doing?" Charles pressed his lips to the back of her hand slowly, his gaze never leaving her eyes. "But if we are to avoid kisses, I will at least take one now." He kissed her hand again. "Or two."

She tried to speak, but it was impossible. How could she when the look of promise in his gaze assured her these kisses would be the first of many? And that those would far outdo a mere kiss on the back of her hand? If that were not enough, she had become fully aware of his arousal pressed against her. At how he'd most certainly bypassed mere friendship and was as eager to experience her as she was him.

"Do it," Abby would likely say. "Pull his lips to yours and see if this is what you think it is. Dear Heavens, sister, what are you waiting for? Seize this grand new adventure with both hands and, most certainly, with your lips!"

Yet she did not. Could not, no matter how much she wanted to. Especially not here, standing in the nursery of his unborn child. So, she reluctantly pulled away yet kept his hand in hers as she urged him to continue their tour. Something he did graciously but with a look on his face that had not been there before. A fresh burst of energy, if she were not mistaken. A new glimmer in his eye that had been lacking until now.

Both of which she felt just as strongly.

Nevertheless, they continued touring, and she remained enraptured by his castle. As mesmerized as she had been since first stepping foot inside its great hall. No, before that. Since she first laid eyes on it from a distance. While shocked Maude had not gushed about what she could expect, she suspected her sister wanted Grace's response to be all for Charles' perusal so he might see firsthand how in love she was with it.

Unequivocally so, at that.

Love at first sight, some might say, as it happened that quickly.

Where MacLauchlin Castle was glorious, its design was more angular and stalwart, likely built initially for defense around a smaller home as clans fought clans more locally. Charles' castle, however, was very much medieval English. While elegant in its own right, it was also built, solid and unbreakable, like its lord. Designed to withstand endless battling from all angles.

Yet inside, much like its master, she saw its weakened spirit.

How neglected it had become without love.

She also saw its perseverance. The affection generations of his family had bestowed on it. Endlessly beautiful craftmanship in nearly every nook and cranny. Unmatchable woodwork most would do anything to have part of their homes.

"Who is that?" Grace wondered at one point in their tour when they came across a life-size portrait that most certainly drew one's eye. She stared up at the vicious-looking armored warrior astride his warhorse and took in the impressive weapons hung on either side of his painting.

"That is a rendition of my great-grandfather many times removed." Charles crossed his arms over his chest and scowled at it. "As ruthless and bloodthirsty as his liege, he was one of Longshanks' most favored and trusted warriors. In fact, he even saved his monarch's life in battle." He gestured at the castle around them. "Because of that, he was titled and given lands and funds to build a castle that would stand strong against our enemies."

"Oh, my." She had not realized. "You mean King Edward the First? He who so despised Sir William Wallace and King Robert the Bruce of Scotland? All Scots, for that matter."

Few British kings were as relentless and sinister as Longshanks. Fewer still who had executed such atrocities against the Scots.

"The one and only." He shook his head. "Hence this being tucked away in a room toward the back."

"I can only imagine." No doubt, it hung here for Charles' love of Blake and Jacob above all. What Scotsman would want to see an ally of such a brutal English king staring down at them when they visited? "Yet still." She contemplated the portrait and saw the pride in the warrior's eyes so clearly reflected in the man standing beside her. "Is he not a symbol of how far your family has come? That you and yours could go from being the sort who defended such terror to a family who would sell off their every heirloom not to 'fill their own coffers' if you will, but to help sustain their people?"

"He is a symbol of something," he replied dryly, considering the portrait. "Though I imagine you must be right and why he still hangs there." He shook his head. "If we are not reminded how far we have come as a nation, our growth is meaningless. Unappreciated." He kept shaking his head. "Yet monsters need not be in the light anymore but in the shadows."

She heard the angst in his voice and spoke to it.

"Or," she offered gently, presenting an alternative, "you could hire an artist to make a much smaller, perhaps drawer-size image if you wish to show it to future generations, then have that same artist replace it with someone you do admire, be they English or Scottish."

"I could." He squeezed her hand. "And likely will, as it is an excellent suggestion."

"Are you sure?" She squeezed his hand back, wanting him to understand she had no intention of overstepping her bounds here. "Because you should do what feels right. Do what makes you happy. And something tells me this ancestor hanging anywhere in your castle does the very opposite. Yet still, you have forfeited much now in the vein of family heirlooms, so it would be understandable if you kept it."

"Yet I keep it for all the wrong reasons." Charles frowned. "Keep it despite feeling judged by it." His eyes leveled on the warrior looking down at him so haughtily. "By him and all his descendants. My forefathers." He might be standing right beside her, but his gaze suddenly seemed far away. Lost. "They fought and suffered in wars just like me, yet I let our castle fall into ruin.

Allowed myself to become a second-hand earl, so to speak, where none of them did any such thing. Rather, they persevered. Rallied on."

"Just as you have," she reminded softly. "And there is nothing second-hand about you. If anything, you strike me as a far better man than the one adorning your wall." She gazed at the warrior again. "In my opinion, your image belongs there far more than his. You are the future of this castle now, not him, and whatever ill-repair it might have fallen into, it is on the mend." Looking his way again, she threaded her fingers with his. "So perhaps now is the perfect time to remove his judging gaze and focus on the future rather than the past."

"My wife would have liked the way you look at things," he murmured, then flinched as if he went too far by mentioning her.

Where some women might be offended, she was not. Rather, she felt honored to be compared to someone he had so adored. She could admit, however, to being curious about his late wife and the life they had shared together. Yet, now did not seem the time to ask about her. Not when comforting him and addressing his concerns seemed far more prevalent.

"No need to flinch when mentioning your late wife, Charles." She rested her hand on his arm and looked him in the eyes. "Part of this, what we hope to find, whether friendship or otherwise, must consist of them, too. My late husband. Your late wife. The pasts we shared with them. At least for now. Perhaps always."

He nodded once as if forcing himself to, and they continued strolling through the castle, leaving his ancestors and talk of their late spouses behind. Nothing more was said about their blossoming feelings or where their marriage might lead. Rather, due to the storm, they spent the remaining day and evening enjoying one another's company.

Determined they began their life here properly, Catlin and Hew chose to eat with those below stairs while she, Charles, and Alexander ate in the dining room. While not nearly the spread they had enjoyed at MacLauchlin Castle, it was delicious, consisting of venison and mixed vegetables. Where she feared Alexander might grow quiet again, he did no such thing.

Then again, how could he when Charles encouraged him to speak and wanted to know everything about him? While William had certainly loved Alexander dearly, she could not recall him spending all that much time talking to him.

Granted, he had been younger, but still.

Alexander had eaten with his nursemaid regularly, and she could not help but wonder why she had not insisted he eat with her and William more often. Perhaps because it was not "done" as a rule, or maybe she had bitten her tongue for the sake of family? What others might think was right? Protocol.

So, she truly enjoyed dinner and conversation with Alexander and Charles and was disappointed when the evening ended, and everyone retired. Even though Charles walked her to her bedroom door like a proper gentleman and tried to bid her goodnight, she did not want to go separate ways just yet. She wanted more time.

"Perhaps a nightcap in front of the fire?" she wondered. "So that we might talk more?"

"We have all the time in the world to talk, my lady." As Charles kissed the back of her hand, his telling gaze flickered from the bed behind Grace to her face. "But tonight is not it, and we both know why."

Before she could deny him, he vanished into the darkened hallway, leaving her to her overheated skin and sensual awareness. Womanly sensations she never thought she would feel again. Frustrating feelings that made her toss and turn well into the night.

Sensations that remained with her right up until morning, through breakfast and into the carriage ride back to MacLauchlin Castle. Like yesterday, there had been a new light in Charles' expression when, certain it would not rain, he sent them on their way.

"I will call on you soon," he assured. "Then we will spend a day in Newcastle and shop."

So, he did, and while eager for time alone with him, he insisted Alexander join them on several of those occasions so he might meet those most important to him. He would see her son feel as much a part of their new life as Grace.

"You say you spent yet another splendid day with Charles, yet you wear a look that worries me," Maude said one night, eyeing Grace over her claret. They were enjoying a nightcap in Blake's study. A small, more cozy area than the drawing room. "What is it, sister? What weighs on your mind?"

"Honestly?" She bit her lower lip and stared into the fire. "It all seems rather too good to be true."

"What?" Maude said, amused. "Rushing into a marriage of convenience to escape my goodwill?" She looked skyward, then gave Grace a knowing look. "Or falling for the man you are determined to remain friends with? One who is positively wonderful with your son?"

"All of the above," she said weakly. "How did you know?"

"About your ever-growing desire for the Earl of Newcastle?" She chuckled. "My dear, it was clear for all to see the moment you laid eyes on him."

"That being clear to you and Lord MacLauchlin alone then," she reminded. "As you were the only two there."

"And the only two needed, I dare say." Maude waved off what she clearly thought a redundant topic. "The moral of the story is you have been mad about each other from the second you stepped foot in the same room." She shrugged. "And it makes sense. It really does. So, when you declared an arranged marriage and mere friendship, I thought, pish-posh, I will believe it when I see it." She gestured at Grace and grinned with triumph. "And now here you have it. You sit here trying to understand how your sad and tortured heart could ever dare love again."

"I am not nearly that far along." But getting closer than she ever thought she might. "I just fear…"

What, exactly? What when everything seemed so perfect? That, she supposed. Smooth waters. Blissful, exciting, romantic waters. Happiness that could too easily hide secrets. A relationship that could perhaps become something it had not been at the beginning.

"I can tell you what you fear," Maude said softly, "but you will not like it."

"Yet you will tell me regardless," she said, knowing her sister all too well.

"If you wish."

"I do not."

"Yet I will."

"As I knew you would."

"You fear William, dear sister." Maude squeezed her hand and looked at her with heartfelt compassion. "Do you not see that yet?"

"I do not understand."

"Perhaps not at face value, but deep down, you do, Grace." Maude gave her hand another squeeze. "And I will tell you why, as you are not ready to see it yourself."

That said, she told Grace something she had long denied but had become more and more conscious of when with Charles. A simple fact that, as her sister had warned, she knew, deep down, might very well be true.

She feared forfeiting her happiness to another husband.

More than that, she feared becoming who she was with William all over again with Charles.

Chapter Ten

It was hard to believe their wedding day had finally arrived without what had become something so perfect taken away. Without Grace ending what was blossoming between them before it had a chance to flourish. Because it was real and powerful, and Charles was already addicted.

In fact, it felt too good to be true, and that worried him.

In his experience, when things grew too pristine in life, it was only a matter of time before everything was ripped away.

"All will be well," Bessie assured him on one of the few nights he had remained home alone. Although his castle and MacLauchlin Castle were only a few hours apart, he and Grace had found spending time together easier if they stayed overnight at one of the two locations. "It is clear Lady Howard is quite taken with you, my lord."

"Be that as it may." He sat before the fire in his study, trying not to fall back into his brooding ways. Dark thoughts. Ones he feared would flare again without Grace around. Whether or not she realized it, she had a way of keeping his spirits lifted. Revived his hope in so much.

Perhaps, too much.

"You cannot live in fear that something will happen to Grace or young Alexander," Bessie had counseled, knowing him well. "Or worry that you might drive them away somehow, for it shall not happen."

What if it did, though? He and Grace had spoken a great deal about many things but perhaps not what they should have most. Their spouses. The melancholy they had suffered from their losses. Not just that, but how it could sometimes be when thoughts of war got the better of him.

Most of all, though, he worried over her not knowing about Blake's incoming business.

While he had not liked waiting until they were married to tell her the truth, he feared her receiving it now would be worse. Their deepening friendship, and perhaps even her heart, would be at risk. A heart that he already cherished more than he could have fathomed. Did he love her? Impossible to know. But it felt like it edged toward that. How could it not when she filled his world with vibrancy and color again?

Their trips to Newcastle and its surrounding villages had been exceptionally bright whether Alexander was along or not. Commoners were far kinder regarding his deformities than the upper crust. There were no uncomfortable stares or haughty attitudes, just hardworking folk happy to see him out and about. Thankfully, Grace and news of their upcoming nuptials were well-received.

Now here they stood, exchanging vows at a small church near his estate.

Grace was, as always, breathtaking. Impossible to look away from. She wore an off-white gown embroidered with delicate silver and blue flowers and a matching bonnet. It all seemed rather surreal when he slipped a ring on her delicate finger and recited his vows: "With this Ring I thee wed, with my body I thee worship, and with all my worldly goods I thee endow: In the Name of the Father, and of the Son, and of the Holy Ghost. Amen."

Then came the kiss. Their very first.

While chaste, he felt the lingering warmth of her lips when he pulled away. Saw the dreamy expression in her eyes that told him she'd enjoyed it every bit as much as he had. That she looked forward to enjoying such again when they were alone. They had held hands over the past few weeks and most certainly flirted, but he'd honored her request and kept things proper, courting her with flowers and even a bauble or two.

Although they would be having a small gathering back at his—*their*—castle, many villagers attended the ceremony. They filled the building and surrounding grounds, cheering their goodwill once Charles and Grace signed the registry and exited the church. Alexander would travel back with the others so they could enjoy a brief respite alone in between. This time, they traveled in his open-air Phaeton carriage to better appreciate the beautiful late autumn day.

Grace smiled and admired her wedding ring. "This is beautiful, Charles."

"I am glad you like it." He met her smile and hoped she liked what it said just as much. "It is inscribed on the inner band."

"Is it?"

She went to remove her ring, but he put his hand over hers before she could. "If you would not mind me simply telling you what it says?" He trailed his fingers along her ring finger. "I rather like seeing your ring just where it is for now."

A gentle, womanly smile curled her mouth as their gazes lingered on one another. "I admit I rather like it there too."

"Good," he murmured, caught in her eyes. In the way she made him feel.

"So, what does it say?" she prompted when he was not forthcoming. Better still, when she realized he had lost his train of thought given the desire simmering between them.

"It says 'To Friendship and All it Entails,' with the date we first met."

Her smile warmed even more. "How perfect."

"I thought so."

"I noticed Bessie packed a small lunch basket." She perked an eyebrow. "Did she not realize we had friends and family arriving after the ceremony?"

"She did but thought on such a lovely day that we might want to stop on the way back and, despite the hour, celebrate with a glass of champagne before spending the afternoon entertaining." He shrugged. "Besides, it will take time for everyone to settle into their rooms. Unless, of course, you would like to get back straight away for your sisters' sake?"

"Oh, I imagine they will be just fine with our delayed arrival." Her cheeks turned rosy. "In fact, I think they would insist on us taking a bit of time alone."

"Excellent." He asked his driver to travel the alternate route home. "Because I know just the spot to take you with a view I think you will appreciate."

"I am most intrigued." She eyed the mix of crimson and rust-colored leaves still lingering on the trees draping over the scarcely used road and seemed to appreciate how the wind scattered dappled sunlight over their surroundings. "How enchanting. A bit of a fairytale route, is it not?"

Peaceful, to be sure. "I suppose one could say that."

They did not go much farther before his driver pulled over. In no mood for decorum and eager to be alone with her, Charles hopped down, helped Grace out, and grabbed the picnic basket.

"Oh, how mysterious," she exclaimed when they started down a narrow, single-file path between tall bushes. "How did you ever find this?"

He stopped, glanced back at her, and wanted to make sure it was not inappropriate. "Might I refer to my late wife on such a day?"

"Absolutely," she said. "You can, anytime you like. You know that. We discussed this." Grace squeezed his hand. "It is something we have not done much of thus far, and I suspect it is because we feared frightening one another off." She held up her ring finger. "Well, we can only go so far now, so never hesitate, Charles. Nor would I ever absolve our friendship or whatnot over talk of Charlotte. Any more than I hope you would over

William."

"Of course not." He continued walking and explained where they were going. "I often walked the woodlands when I returned from war. Not just to escape the heartache of losing my family but as a means to cope with memories of battle. A relentless melancholy of sorts. That is when I discovered where I am bringing you now."

"I remain intrigued." She hesitated a moment. "Do you still suffer such heartache and melancholy?"

"As to my family, quite often before you and I met."

"And your memories of war?" she prompted when he did not go on because he feared what she might think.

"Not gone altogether, I am afraid." He kept walking rather than glancing back. "Hopefully someday."

She offered no response, but he suspected she thought about it. Wondered what that might mean for them. Perhaps even for Alexander.

"Oh, my," she whispered, awed when the path opened to a flat, moss-covered rock ledge that overlooked the sweeping sea and their castle in the distance. "How utterly lovely. It looks like something out of a painting." She glanced from the gold and red leaves on the tree limbs overhead to the thick shrubs on either side. She glanced from the tree limbs overhead to the thick foliage on either side. "A peaceful alcove, indeed."

"It has been." He pulled a blanket out of the basket and laid it on the ground before pouring two small glasses of champagne. "A place I could get away from all the memories yet still see them from afar." He sat down beside her. "Remember a home I never thought I would return to when I went off to war. It allowed me just the right amount of distance, I suppose. I could pretend…"

"I understand more than you can imagine," Grace said when he trailed off. She threaded her fingers with his and gazed at the castle. "Thank you for bringing me here, Charles. For trusting me with a location that I imagine you have kept most secret. A spot that is all yours."

It had been, but now he wanted it to be hers, too.

"Here is to our arrangement, Lady Newcastle." While odd calling another woman by that title, he did not find it disagreeable. Not at all. Eager for what lay ahead, hopefully, that very night, he tipped his glass against hers. "Might it be everything we hoped?"

"To our arrangement," she returned softly. "And friendship, amongst other things."

That sounded promising.

"Anytime you want to come here, do not hesitate," he said when her gaze returned to the castle. He sipped his champagne and admired not the view but her. How beautiful she looked surrounded by nature. By anything, for that matter.

"I will, thank you." Even though her attention seemed absorbed in the view as she sipped her drink as well, it seemed her mind was just as much on him. "You should know that William had a few friends who fought in the war, too. One never came home, but the other did. He was much changed, however."

Grace set aside her cup, looked at him most seriously, and wrapped her free hand around their adjoined hands. "He suffered an affliction that could often take him back to wartime. A deep, sometimes frightening, melancholy. An inability to separate the past from the present, I suppose." Clearly needing to understand, she eyed him curiously. "Does that sound familiar, Charles?"

Too much so. Frighteningly so, some might say. "What would you say if it does?"

"As your wife and friend, I would say that I am here for you," she replied without hesitation. "Always here for you, no matter how dark things might get on occasion."

Even though kinder words had never been spoken, he still feared. Not for him but for her. Perhaps even for Alexander. "While I appreciate that, I will not have you or your son near me if such occurs. Nor would Mrs. Bessie or Mr. Thomas as they have developed an eye for such coming before it arrives."

"Has it happened since we met?"

"No." He shook his head. "Though I came close a few times on those rare nights we were apart."

"Then perhaps I am helpful?" She cocked her head. "And might continue to be so, as I can tell you now, I will not have you shut away from me if you are suffering. Alexander, yes." She shook her head. "But not me. That is not what friendship, at the very least, is about. To that end, despite it being our wedding day," her voice grew gentler and coaxing, "might you tell me what happened? Because from what I understand, afflictions such as yours tend to center around a singular traumatic event."

While admittedly, it was the last thing he wanted to talk about on such a day, he understood her need to know, so he thought about how to describe it without losing himself in it. How to scratch the surface.

"You are correct," he began, still seeing the enemy flags looming on the horizon. "While I fought in several battles afoot and on water, it was a particularly vicious high seas battle against the Americans, who, as you know, were allied with the French during the war, that..." *How to say it? Simply, he supposed.* "That finally wounded both my flesh and mind."

When he paused to gather himself, she squeezed his hand, waited, and looked at him with compassion he was not sure he deserved.

"Suffice it to say, we were en route to lend aid to our own but did not anticipate how numerous the American ships. How vastly outnumbered we would be." He could still hear the roar of cannon fire in the distance. See bright red flames against a darkening sky. "And I manned the largest ship rather than the faster ones in what soon became a rescue mission."

"Good God," she said softly, understanding more than he anticipated about naval warfare. "You became a wall between the Americans and British."

"Indeed," he said softly, still seeing the resolved faces of his men when they realized what they had to do. "Yet all were willing to sacrifice their lives for their countrymen. For fellow navy so they might live to fight another day."

"And how many did?" She blinked back tears. "How many did you lose, Charles?"

"Too many." He still felt the sway of his ship as they fired cannon after cannon at the enemy. Felt the jerk of the hull and vibration underfoot as cannonballs slammed into them in return. Smelled the acrid gunpowder and the metallic scent of blood.

Heard the cries of death.

Choked on and struggled to see through the cloying eye-watering smoke.

"In the end, I lost over half my crew." He still searched them out in his mind. Peered through the smoke and flames to locate them. "I carried as many as I could find and handed them off to the crewman on the next ship, but it was not enough. Far from enough. Then the stars and stripes were right there, and I was fighting hand and fist to save my men. After that, everything went hazy until I awoke in England scarred and minus an eye."

"I am so very sorry, Charles." Grace rested her head on his shoulder. "But know this. You *were* enough, and I suspect every life you saved that day thought so."

Whether they did or not, he would always carry the weight of being unable to save everyone. Of having to sacrifice their lives to begin with.

He and Grace sat silently for a while, and he was grateful for it. Not because he felt his mind going deeper into the dark hole of times gone by but because she lent him peace. Freed him of his demons in some unexplainable way. Yet still, they were demons that could rear their ugly heads anytime, so he redirected their conversation to what they had been talking about before.

"Did you ever see your husband's friend experience his post-war melancholy firsthand?" he wondered.

"I did not, but William did." Grace lifted her head and looked at him. "He claimed it was both heartbreaking and terrifying." Her compassionate gaze never left his face. "That you have suffered such saddens me more than you know. So, I *will* be there for you no matter how hard you might try to push me away."

While tempted to deny her, now was not the time. Rather, now was the moment to appreciate that such a caring, lovely woman had come into his life. One he could no longer imagine remaining mere friends with. So, he set aside his glass, cupped her cheek, and finally did what he had wanted to do for some time and kissed her.

Not a quick, friendly kiss by any means but one he had not given another since Charlotte. Yet it was not the same. Could not be when this was a different woman. A different experience entirely when her mouth opened to his, and their kiss deepened and grew more passionate. Became something in which he lost himself. Something that showed him in one fell swoop that friendship would be the very least of what they shared.

A certainty that both delighted and terrified him enough to end the kiss, albeit gradually. "I fear if we do not stop now, we will keep our guests waiting far too long."

"Quite right," she whispered hoarsely. Her dewy, feminine gaze lingered on his face. "In the vein of being honest, though I do so love my kin, I wish we had your castle all to ourselves upon our return."

"*Our* castle." He could not help caressing her soft cheek a moment longer before he pulled away and finished his champagne. "And I much agree. However, they are awaiting us, and I am sure they are eager to see you."

As it happened, he was right.

Her sisters were gathered in the great hall when they arrived home a short while later. One sister, in particular, was more eager to see her than the others. A sibling they were not sure would be able to make it due to an elderly husband with good and bad days.

"Abby!" Grace exclaimed when they walked through the front door.

"Dear, beautiful sister, *there* you are." Lady Abigail flew into Grace's waiting arms like they had not seen each other in ages.

"How I have missed you!"

Grace had spoken at length about her sisters but probably most about her youngest sibling, Abby. A vivacious beauty with crimson locks, one could see by the excitement in her eyes that she was every bit the adventuresome spirit Grace had claimed.

"I have missed you too, my darling sister." Grace embraced Abby, beaming. "I did not think you would make it." She glanced around. "Is Lord Somerset with you?"

"He is but resting at the moment, I am afraid." Abby glanced Charles' way. "And provided a downstairs chamber by your gracious new husband, which I most appreciate."

"Oh, yes, you two *must* finally meet." Grace introduced them. "I have told you both a great deal about each other, so I do hope you get on well."

"I cannot see why we would not." Abby was not shy about looking him over, her tongue every bit as bold as he had heard. "My, you are dashing, are you not, Lord Newcastle?" She issued a rather saucy smile, and her knowing gaze slid from Grace back to him. "Absolutely perfect for my sister. A grand adventure I suspect she will enjoy for many years to come."

Prudence muffled a chuckle, Maude snapped out her fan, and Grace turned red.

"Lady Somerset." He bowed from the waist. "A pleasure to meet another one of Lady Newcastle's lovely sisters."

One who was clearly a handful.

"Likewise." Abby clasped Grace's hand and smiled back and forth between them. "I so wish we had arrived in time to see you exchange vows, but I am glad we are here for breakfast and celebrations."

"As are we, my lady." He looked from Grace to Abby with a warm smile. The sort that seemed to come more and more naturally nowadays. "Very much so."

Everyone visited for a bit before adjourning to the dining room just after noon to enjoy his castle's grandest spread in ages. Everything from freshly baked rolls, buttered toast, eggs, ham, and bacon to a variety of freshly caught fish and, of course, their wedding cake for dessert. Naturally, he insisted Alexander join them and sat Grace on his right side and the boy on his left. It might be unorthodox, but he could care less. He liked the boy's company and would have him with them on such an important occasion.

"Have you enjoyed the day so far, Alexander?" he asked at one point. "And are you all moved into your new room?"

"I have, and I am, my lord." Where Alexander might have hesitated to say more before, he continued with a small, co-conspirator smile. "And I very much look forward to becoming more familiar with your castle."

"*Our* castle." He met the boy's smile. "And we shall resume our tour first thing tomorrow."

"Well, perhaps not *first* thing, nephew," Abby piped up, shameless when she winked at Grace, yet still couth enough to cover her tracks. "I was hoping you might show me this impressive room of yours and perhaps give me a tour around the parts of this magnificent medieval structure you have already explored."

"Of course, my lady." Alexander nodded once, like the little lord he was becoming. "It would be my honor."

After they finished eating, Grace begged a few minutes alone with her sisters to refresh herself before they resumed celebrating. Where they were initially going to do so in the ballroom, they had decided the sizable piano room and its attached terrace would be a better choice so people could enjoy the brisk but sunny weather.

"Come." Jacob clasped his shoulder and looked from Blake to Charles. "Let us take this time to toast your marriage, old chap."

"Do you not mean *arrangement*?" Blake teased as they made their way into Charles' study. He chuckled and shook his head. "Though I suspect our friend sees it as much more than that now."

"Perhaps," he said vaguely, not about to admit it just yet.

"Perhaps?" Jacob met Blake's chuckle and shook his head as MacLauchlin presented a well-aged and costly bottle of whisky. "Deny it all you like, but what you share with your lovely new wife is apparent to all, and it is well beyond friendship."

Were they that obvious? He supposed they must be. After all, they had set out to be most genuine, had they not? Something that had come remarkably easy. And while he'd meant to keep denying it, especially with these two and their We Told You So attitudes, he suddenly felt foolish. They were his oldest friends and wanted to see him happy.

"I confess things between Lady Grace, and I have progressed further than I anticipated." He nodded thanks when Blake handed him a glass of whisky. "She is…" *What? A welcome addition to his life? More kind-hearted than he probably deserved? Utterly perfect?* "A treasure, if I were to be honest." He shook his head in disbelief that she was his. They were one another's. "Something, *someone*, I never expected. A most welcome presence I did not think I would experience again in this life."

"Then here is to unexpected welcome presences." Jacob held up his glass and smiled. "And things you never thought you would feel again."

Blake raised his glass and smiled as well. "Here, here!"

He held up his whisky in thanks and drank, eager for the rest of the day. Desperate for it. Would things progress as he hoped? Or, when the time finally came, would one of them find they could only go so far?

Chapter Eleven

ALMOST AS IF her feet did not touch the ground, Grace felt like she walked on thin air as she joined her sisters upstairs to refresh herself. Had she felt this way with William when they married? Surely. The years in-between must have altered that feeling as time tended to do.

Or perhaps it was more as Maude had concluded that day in Blake's study when she urged Grace to confess her marriage had been more problematic than she was willing to admit. While she deeply loved William, she was terrified she might grow overly tolerant again. That her soft heart could very well fall victim to accepting another man's habits or quirks, as it were.

Charles claimed he loathed gambling, so there was comfort in that, but still. She kept meaning to voice her added concerns but repeatedly bit her tongue. Especially when he took her to his special place overlooking the sea. How could she confess her worries when she realized the true extent of his post-war struggles?

When she learned what he had gone through in war to begin with.

Now, it seemed impossible to tell him she feared forfeiting her happiness to her husband's problems. Granted, there was a marked difference between a gambling addiction and the sort of melancholy war veterans suffered, but it could very well take the same toll on someone who cared about them. Somebody determined to stand by them no matter what. Because as selfish as it may sound, there was great pain to be had on both fronts. She suspected watching William's angst as he struggled to fight the demons ruining his family and the sorts of inner beasts Charles battled with were capable of equal ruin.

Either way, she had decided to keep her concerns firmly in the back of her mind for the time being. A task easily accomplished when Charles kissed her. Where his kiss at the altar had filled her with undeniable anticipation, the one he bestowed in their spot made things come alive in her that had long been dormant.

Perhaps even made new things spring to life.

"I do not think I have ever seen you look so beautiful, sister," Maude said as Catlin removed Grace's bonnet. Her sisters lounged nearby, enjoying a glass of claret and, by all appearances, admiring her.

"I could not agree more." Prudence smiled. "You positively shine, Grace."

"She really does." Abby wore a dreamy expression while Catlin removed hairpins. "Like a woman well-satisfied."

Catlin smoothed the way when Maude and Prudence smirked, and Grace blushed even though she had nothing to blush over.

"I agree. You have never been more beautiful, my lady." Her friend styled her hair into a fashion better suited to no bonnet and smiled at her in the mirror. "I wish you many years of happiness with Lord Newcastle. He is a fine gentleman indeed."

Maude tipped her glass in agreement. "To a lifetime of happiness, to be sure."

"And love," Prudence echoed, tipping her glass as well. She eyed Grace with approval. "Because such has been found already in this arrangement of yours, has it not?"

"Oh, something has been found, all right." Abby winked at Grace and added her toast to the mix. "And I truly could not be happier for you, dear sister, for none deserves what you have found more than you."

"You mean rediscovered," Grace said.

"No, I mean *found.*" Abby was by far the bluntest of them, which said something. "As I suspect the love you have with Charles will be different than what you felt for William, may he rest in peace. I loved my brother by marriage, but they are men of a different cut, and I imagine it is only a matter of time before you figure that out."

"Abby." Prudence frowned. "You go too far."

"Yet I say what we are all thinking." Abby closed the distance, crouched before Grace, took her hands, and looked at her with unabashed affection. "I am sorry, but it is time someone said this. May you take it with the love in which it is intended." She shook her head. "While there can be no doubt William cared dearly for you in his own way, it was not real love. Not unconditional love. If it were, he would have put you and our dear Alexander first always. Put you before the thrill of betting coin he had not earned. A rush that took precedence and nearly ruined you all."

"Must we do this right now?" she said, growing upset. "On my wedding day?"

"I think perhaps it is the best day to do it." Prudence joined them and rested a comforting hand on Grace's shoulder. "Because this is the first day of a much different marriage with a much different man."

"Is he, though?" she said softly, saying more than she intended. "When he is wounded far more deeply than what one can see physically?"

"But not wounded beyond repair." Maude seemed to understand as she joined them, rested her hand on Grace's other shoulder, and squeezed it in reassurance. "Blake has told me about Charles' post-war horrors. The bouts of melancholy that can come upon him." She shook her head. "But that is not the same as what William suffered, dear sister. Not remotely. Charles' inner demons are not born of selfishness but selflessness.

They are much different creatures."

"They very much are." Prudence crouched beside Abby and looked at Grace with compassion. With the same support, they all did. "To that end, we are happier than you can imagine that you are letting Charles into your heart because we suspect he will cherish it in ways you cannot yet fathom."

"So, might you enjoy your beautiful wedding day." Maude offered Grace a soft, loving smile. "Because I do not doubt it will remain in your memories and hearts until your dying breath."

"I could not agree more, and I have known the man mere minutes beyond your letters." Abby wiped a tear from Grace's cheek. "Yet I need but a moment to assess one's character to get it quite right." Her eyebrow swept up. "And your Charles? Someone truly rare. Someone to be most cherished."

"I believe he very much is," she said, her voice choppy with emotion. In truth, she felt both terrified and excited about where her heart was taking her. The leap she suspected it had already made.

A leap that became thunder in her ears every time she and Charles were close the remainder of the day. While theirs was a small gathering, everything was lovely, from the dancing to the torches Charles insisted be lit on the terrace, lending an old-world feel to a vibrant sunset.

"This day has been most memorable," Charles murmured in her ear from behind. He placed his hands on the railing on either side of her as the moon rose. "But I admit that I long for time alone. To kiss you once again, if you will allow such?"

Allow such? It was all she had been able to think about for the better part of the day. Since the last time he'd pressed his lips to hers. Since she had felt a sweet ache blossom between her thighs that would not abate.

"I would very much like that, husband." Rather than turn, she leaned back against him and enjoyed the warmth of his body. "When do you think it appropriate to make our escape?"

Bessie had seen Alexander upstairs some time ago for more

model-making, so she need not worry about his welfare. From what she could tell, he had enjoyed himself and was, without doubt, fond of Charles. Vice versa, too, by how her husband had spent time chatting with him when most would not on their wedding day.

"I think it would have been appropriate to make our escape hours ago." He kissed the top of her head. "Mr. Thomas saw food and drink brought to my room, so we could go there for a time if you wish."

"For a time?" She closed her eyes to the feel of his hands resting over hers on the railing. At how his arm felt when it came around her waist to brace them against the wind that seemed endless here. "Or perhaps longer?"

"I think we both already know the answer to that."

She suspected they did but still felt self-conscious and shy when he took her hand and led her up a back way to his room. A small, cozy fire already crackled on the hearth when they entered, and numerous candles cast a warm glow. An iced bottle of champagne sat on a table in a decorated silver bucket, along with various snacks.

While tempted to talk, perhaps touch on what she and her sisters had spoken of earlier, any potential words vanished when he shut the door and swept her into his arms. More pointedly, when he cupped the back of her neck and kissed her so passionately, all her concerns melted away.

So much so that she hardly felt him work his nimble fingers and lower her dress. Nimble fingers still as he peppered kisses down the side of her neck and untied her stays. She had no idea how much progress he had made until her dress was pooled around her feet, her corset tossed aside, and she was in nothing but her chemise as he knelt before her.

"What are you doing?" she said in a strangled whisper.

"Adoring you," he said just as hoarsely as he wrapped his arms around her and rested his cheek against her belly. "Cherishing you."

She rested her hands on his head and closed her eyes to the feel of him holding her like this. Loving her like this. It was different from anything she had experienced before, and she liked it immensely. Somehow it felt arousing and supportive all at once. Intimate and sensual at the same time.

Especially when he removed her shoes and explored.

"Oh," she half gasped, half crooned when he, bit by bit, ran his hands up the back of her thighs until he rolled down each stocking one by one, dusting his fingers over her bared skin. More so indeed, when he looked up at her with so much desire, she struggled for breath.

"It will not be long now, my lady," he murmured, tossing aside her stockings. She could see the barely constrained tension in his face and body and felt the same.

Had she ever felt so horribly, wonderfully aware? Every little thing felt pronounced, from the cool air dusting her nether region, making her acutely conscious of her vulnerability, to the growing ache between her thighs that made her knees weak and her legs tremble.

"Do you understand?" he prompted, rather firm now about what was coming.

Deliciously wicked anticipation rolled through her. "I believe I do, my lord."

"Good."

She gasped when he scooped her under the thighs until she straddled his waist and brought her down on the bed at an angle. He yanked up her chemise, settled between her thighs, and made her grab the bedpost over her head when he kissed her not passionately but hungrily.

In a way she had never been kissed before.

She met his desperation. The wild twist of his tongue around hers. It almost seemed that the winds howling outside gusted straight through her soul as they struggled to get closer, desperate to be part of each other in some unexplainable way. Not just sensually but deeper, as if they battled to find something lost to them.

"Charles," she gasped, needing more, pulsing in places she never had before. Outright throbbing. "Where are you?"

She had no idea why she asked, what she needed, what they *both* needed, only that her desperation had become too much. Blistering and overwhelming.

"Charles." Cupping his cheeks, she brought his gaze to her face and made sure he understood just how much she wanted this. Had to have it right away. "Please, husband." She nodded once, confident he would understand something even she did not. "Now is the time."

His gaze stayed with hers for a stretched moment, during which neither seemed able to catch their breath before he reached down and freed himself. She moaned when he stroked the overly sensitive flesh between her thighs with his fingers without taking his gaze from her. Clutching the bedpost with one hand and his shoulder with the other, she pressed up into his touch as he built her up more than she already was.

She bit her lower lip and twisted her hand into the front of his shirt when she grew close to cresting. Gasped what she wanted. "Not like this…"

He seemed to understand because he brushed his lips across hers, grabbed the bedpost above her hand, seized her hip with his free hand, and pressed forward. She tried to keep her eyes on his, loved the raw intimacy, but it was impossible to focus as his hard length stretched and filled her.

She had little grasp on what happened after that because too many sensations washed over her. Intense feelings spiraled from her head right down to her toes when he filled her completely, released a ragged groan of approval, and started moving.

Really moving.

Not just thrusting but grinding and rolling his hips in a way that made her cry out every time. Groan with every hard or even minuscule shift of his hips because each thrust was different. Varied. Better than the last. He offered her so much pleasure that she arched against him, desperate for what built between them because it was not the sort of release to which she was accustomed. She was certain of it. Knew it with every ounce of her being. Every last drop of her soul.

"Charles," she sobbed, clawing at him to come closer. Sweat broke out on her brow, she clenched the post harder and struggled to drag in air.

"Grace," he half-gasped, half-growled. "Should I…do you…"

"Yes." She appreciated that he worried about a potential pregnancy, but she was too close. Wanted this with him no matter what came of it. Found herself desperate for what, or *who*, they might create together but could not find the strength to wrap her legs around him to hold him in place.

She already shook too hard.

Had lost too much control.

Whether Charles wanted the same, the child that might result from this coupling, he seemed just as much a prisoner as she, and thrust harder. Once, twice, then a third time before he buried himself deep and locked up against her.

She kept struggling to drag in air when her body tightened almost unbearably, followed by an exquisite pleasure that invoked a ragged cry. Clinging to him, she shuddered…and shuddered. Gave into a release that made her desperate to inhale his scent. Flicked her tongue over his salty, taxed skin. Everything she'd just experienced in his arms felt primal and different and so perfect that she was gone.

Lost in a way she had never been before.

They stayed that way for a time, their hearts pounding against each other's, and their bodies locked together in a way that remained arousing even after it should not have been. Eventually, they eased apart, but their passion remained when he finally lifted his head, and their gazes caught once more.

As sated as she might be, she wanted more. It seemed he did, too, because the soft kiss he dropped on her lips soon turned to many kisses before he swelled inside her again.

"Roll over," she murmured against his lips, wanting control this time. "Let me straddle you."

When he did as asked, she bit her lower lip again at how good this new position felt. She had only ever done it once with William, but it was toward the end of their marriage, and her mind had been distracted by finances. So, the act had been awkward rather than fulfilling.

Charles was not William, though. Rather, he seemed intensely interested in how she would proceed. He watched her with such intense desire and approval that any inhibitions she suffered vanished, and she felt rather daring.

Sensual.

Eager to please him.

So, she placed his hands on her thighs and urged him to touch her. Feel her. And he did, running his hands up her legs slowly. He dusted his thumbs so close to her center that his member leapt inside her, and she jolted with awareness.

Never taking his gaze off her, his hands crawled beneath her chemise on either side of her waist until stopping just beneath her breasts. Once again, she struggled for breath when the fingers of one hand swirled lightly over her belly, igniting sharp shivers of pleasure while his other hand caressed first one breast and then the other.

Drowning in the way he made her feel, the confidence and sensuality he brought out in her, she slowly, inch by inch, pulled her chemise over her head and tossed it aside. His pupils flared in approval, and he licked his lips ever-so-slightly as he took her in. Licked his lips as though he envisioned tasting everything he looked at. In turn, she ran her hand up beneath his tunic, only for him to grab her wrist and frown.

Not with anger but alarm.

"What is it?" she said, sure to keep her tone soft and accepting.

"You should not." He shook his head. "It will take from the moment."

"Might I be the judge of that, husband?" she said gently. While what they had done thus far could still fall within the confines of good friendship and fulfilling their bodily needs, she would be a fool to say she did not want more at this point.

All of him.

Every last bit.

So she said what needed saying. "Might I see all of you, for I would cherish it as I do you."

Charles clenched his jaw, and his breathing picked up again. A vein ticked in his temple as their gazes held, and he appeared to weigh just how ready he was for this. More specifically, what she might think when she saw him. He almost seemed a warrior preparing to face off with all that was coming at him.

Yet still, thankfully, he eventually nodded curtly and sat up enough to pull off his tunic.

While determined to show no emotion, her vision blurred at the angry scars marring his broad chest. Whatever happened after his mind went hazy fighting off the Americans, he had clearly put up a good fight.

Moreover, he had fought them until what should have been his bitter end.

While she could not empathize with what he had felt then, she could ensure how he felt now. And that was, above all, to feel desired. Loved. So, she ran her fingers over his scars gently, then peppered tender kisses in the wake of her touch. Moved her hips slowly so he would not focus on his wounds, or the memories attached to them but the sensations she wrung from him.

Eventually, she kissed her way up his neck, along his scarred cheek, until she touched his patch, only for him to grab her wrist again and shake his head. He tried to speak, explain why he was not ready, but she put a finger to his lips and tried to ease his struggle.

"I understand," she said softly, with all the care in her heart. She cupped his cheeks and never looked away from him. Not for an instant. "Let us be just as we are. Who we are."

Determined to pull him away from the unrest growing in his gaze, one not entirely part of this moment, she continued moving. Craving more intimacy, she rested her body against his and nuzzled her cheek into his neck as she rode him. Gave him pleasure even as she received it. Hoped she would be able to handle his inner war wounds because she had just glimpsed them, and they were very real.

So real, she feared she would not be enough.

More so, that she might lose herself trying to prove she was.

Chapter Twelve

"I AM HERE, love," Charles managed, his voice guttural even to his own ears as he struggled with Grace seeing the scars on his chest for the first time. Troubled because she had wanted to see beneath his patch. Caught somewhere between the past and present as most of his wounds were laid bare.

Far away yet right here all at once.

Here with his beautiful, perfect wife who straddled him and tried her best not to look worried as she rested against his chest. Did her best not to fear that he might be back in a battle she had no control over. How else could it be when he had allowed her to see so much? Not just the physical aspects, either, but his inner emotions. The unrest in his gaze when she tried to remove his patch and reveal a wound that made him feel ugly and broken.

A terrible flaw no woman should have to suffer.

"I am here," he repeated, returning to the sensations she pulled from him. How good her stunning body felt against his. The gripping heat of her tight sheath.

While tempted to wrap his arms around her and thrust until he let go again, he feared releasing inside her once more. He could hardly believe he had done so already when a child could very well mean facing catastrophic loss again. But she had felt so incredible. So impossible to free himself from.

A mistake he did not intend to make twice.

First, though, she needed to see he was well, so he rocked her back until she had no choice but to brace her hands on his chest and look at him. See that he was all right and not going down the dark path he had warned her about.

"Do you see me, wife?" He cupped her cheek. "Do you understand I am well?" When her lower lip wobbled in uncertainty, he did all he could to show her he was in the present rather than the past. He rubbed the tiny nub at the apex of her pleasure with the pad of his thumb and kept with honesty. "While I went somewhere else for a moment, I am no longer there but right here with you. Only ever with you."

"Truly?" she managed breathlessly, caught somewhere between concern and building pleasure.

"Yes." He groaned at how good she felt and nudged his hips up enough to let her know he craved movement and was desperate to feel more. What he did not expect was how desperate she was too. How well she would move once she was certain he was all right. How incredible not just the act would feel but watching her take her pleasure. Up. Down. Swirling her hips. Grinding. Entrenched in her emotions. Angry and excited all at once if he did not know better.

It took everything in him not to grab her backside, sit up and squeeze her against him so hard they both sailed over the edge, but he understood she needed this. So, he clenched the bedding, tried to hold on, and not let go inside her.

Time it just right.

An outright impossibility when she dug her nails into his skin, ground especially deep, and whimpered in pleasure. Imprisoned by the feel of her, the sheer ecstasy she invoked, he jerked and let go as well. And kept letting go as she melted down against him. Despite frustration that he released inside her again, he was glad to have her close once more, so he wrapped his arms around her and held her.

Never wanted to let her go.

Grace was so different from Charlotte in how she made him

feel. Freed him in a way his late wife never could. Would Charlotte have been so compassionate? Yes, always on her good days. Grace, however, would prove constant, and he found himself looking forward to it. Eager to experience life with her. While fearful she could become pregnant and history would repeat itself, he was desperate to be with her always. To feel such inner warmth drive away the darkened shadows of his mind and experience the untouchable emotion he knew full well was love.

Deep, profound love he feared ever losing.

At some point, he must have drifted off because the next thing he knew, he woke, and she was gone. He was back on his ship for a moment, and everyone he was trying to save was impossible to find. Vanished and lost to him.

He bolted upright only to discover the day's first rays streaming through the window. Confused, as he slept lighter than most, he frowned, worried, until he spied a note from Grace on the bedside table. Alexander was an early riser, so she wanted to be downstairs when he woke for breakfast on his first morning here. She had also requested that Thomas let Charles sleep in.

While he understood her reasoning, something about it felt off. Abby had made it clear she would see to Alexander this morning, so why did Grace feel such a need? Did she not want to wait for him to wake the day after their wedding? Perhaps make love one more time?

Because Lord knew he did, despite the pleasure he had already found in her arms.

Trying to keep in mind they had come to a mutual agreement that did not commit her to love but rather friendship and matters of the flesh, he got out of bed and dressed. When he arrived downstairs, there were scant few up, given the hour. Alexander was nowhere to be seen, and Grace and Abby sat next to an old man in a gouty chair so he might be wheeled around.

"Good morning, my new brother by marriage." Abby smiled from the elderly man to Charles. "Darling, meet Grace's new husband, Charles, Earl of Newcastle."

In turn, she introduced her spouse as Reginald, Viscount of Somerset.

He had heard of the man and his esteemed family name. They went back further than most, and none were so proudly English. Reginald might not hold the highest of titles, but that mattered little. His lineage traced back to William the Conqueror, which made him and his kin important.

"A pleasure to meet you, Lord Somerset." Although his station was above Reginald's, one must honor those English families that withstood the test of time. Therefore, while he did not bow, he lowered his head and acknowledged Abby's husband as one of his own. "I hope your stay has been satisfactory thus far."

"Well, if I were honest, it is a damn dusty castle and," Reginald grunted only to fall into a coughing fit.

"Shh, my dear," Abby cooed, resting her hand on his back. In fact, she showed more compassion than anticipated when she held a napkin to Somerset's mouth and shielded him the best she could from Charles and Grace. Not out of embarrassment for herself based on her softly spoken words of support, but to spare his dignity as his coughs abated.

"Come, husband." Grace did not greet Charles with the same warm smile her sister had but seemed rather detached when she steered him out of the room. "Alexander is still resting, so I was going to come back upstairs but changed my mind. Instead, I decided to wait for you so we might take a stroll and talk."

"A stroll?" He tensed, sensing something amiss. "At this hour the day after our wedding? Even you must understand how—"

"How what?" she said softly. "How it might be at odds with the actions of a loving wife despite our arrangement stipulating nothing more than friendship?" Anger flashed in her eyes. "And I dare say a questionable friendship at that."

"What is it, Grace?" He grew tenser by the moment. "What troubles you?"

Unfortunately, she had no time to respond before Prudence and Jacob came downstairs.

"How lovely." Prudence smiled. "I had no idea anyone other than us enjoyed a stroll at this hour." Her smile faltered when she realized Grace seemed out of sorts. "I can only imagine that is why you are down here so early the morning after your wedding?"

"Actually, I arose to check on Alexander but ended up spending time with Abby and Lord Somerset instead." There was no missing now that Grace was upset about something. "Might we all stroll together, as I would like to speak with you two just as much as I would my husband."

"Of course." Prudence glanced from Jacob to Charles warily. "Let us get our coats."

So they did and stepped out into the chilly morning. Unlike MacLauchlin Castle, this one did not have as many areas to walk outside without having to navigate steep paths threading down through the cliffs. So Charles led them along the less windy side of the castle to a sitting area overlooking the sea.

"What is it, sister?" Prudence asked once they arrived. "What did you wish to speak with us about?"

"Well, as it happens, Lord Somerset revealed something just before Charles came downstairs." Grace frowned from him to the others. "Something he seemed quite surprised I did not know as it is apparently common knowledge."

His heart sank at the hurt in her eyes.

"I can only hope he was wrong," Grace continued, "but based on Abby's troubled expression at the time, I suspect he was not." She looked from the others to Charles. "Is it true Lord MacLauchlin offered to bring his shipping business to the port of the man I chose to marry? That I was a prize not only because of a generous dowry, but primarily because of said business?"

Sorry that he had not told her yet, Charles cursed under his breath. He should have shared this critical information with her the moment they married as he had intended. But now, he could see by the pain and anger in her gaze that it was too late.

To that end, he would give her the honesty she had deserved

from the beginning.

"It is true," he said softly. "And I cannot tell you how sorry I am for not telling you sooner."

"I cannot tell you how sorry I am, too," she said, wounded. "As our friendship was supposed to be built on honesty. On…" she broke off and visibly gathered herself before looking at the other two. Specifically, her sister. "So, you knew? Both of you?" Her cheeks flamed red as the enormity of it hit her. "Maude and clearly Abby as well?" She shook her head. "*All* of you knew, and nobody said a word?"

"Charles wanted to," Prudence said, determined to defend him first, it seemed. "He was quite defiant about it, but we begged him not to. We worried you would reject him because of it and make a hasty decision that might have landed you and Alexander in an unfortunate marriage instead."

"An *unfortunate* marriage?" Grace's eyebrows shot up, and the corners of her mouth slashed down. "How could you think I would risk that? No matter what, I would have kept my son's best interests in mind when marrying again." Her gaze narrowed. "Moreover, what gave you the right to take that decision out of my hands in the first place?" She rounded her eyes. "Do you think me that incapable of seeing after myself? After Alexander?"

"We thought you wounded as you so clearly were, and it broke our hearts," Prudence said gently. "Jacob, Blake, and Maude were equally worried about Charles, so they thought you a good match." She gave Grace a pointed look. "And they were proved right almost straight away. After that, we could not risk you turning him away out of mere pride. Tell me if I am wrong? Tell me your sole reason for remarrying again was anything other than you not wanting to feel beholden to Blake and Maude? You cannot because that is the reason you wanted to remarry. Your pride had already gotten the better of you. You know it, and we know it."

"It should have been my choice whether I would have or not." Grace's jaw tightened as she considered the three of them.

"Did any of you consider the consequences of not telling me?" She wiped away a tear and homed in on Charles. "Now, how can I ever be certain our friendship is genuine, let alone the validity of any other feelings you might have for me when you were undoubtedly focused on a much grander prize?" Her gaze cut back to Prudence, and she went for the jugular. "Furthermore, for all you worried over my state of mind dealing with William's gambling addiction, why would you wish me to be with a man who was equally neglectful with money?"

Charles flinched at that but deserved it because she was right. He had been, and it almost cost him everything.

"You know full well why Charles was neglectful with his funds," Prudence countered. "And while yes, some might use the word 'neglectful', I would argue selling off one's inheritance to keep the villagers afloat should stand for something. Speak to his character, if nothing else. That aside, it should be noted he was very responsible before everything he suffered. Successful, even."

"I would not know," Grace fumed. "As that is yet another thing we have not discussed." She frowned at Charles. "But then, as with all men, why would you ever talk finances with a woman?"

Before he could respond, she spun on her heel and stormed off. Desperate to assuage her anger, he caught up with her on the pathway.

"Grace, wait." He grabbed her hand and stopped her. "Please let me explain because I could not be sorrier. You must believe me when I tell you how much I wanted to reveal this to you sooner. How much it upset me not to."

"Yet you managed, which tells me you agreed with my sisters that I am too prideful." Grace shook her head. "Then, when you finally had the chance, you did not. Rather you—" she swallowed hard—"allowed intimacy with such a profound lie between us. Worse still, allowed my feelings for you to grow. Made me care." She wiped away another tear, freed her hand, and backed away. "Now, how can I ever trust you again? More sadly still, as I said before, how can I ever believe your feelings, whether platonic or otherwise, are genuine?"

"Because we are married now," he said bluntly. "And I still feel the same." He made things clear. "Actually, I feel much more. Far more. Rest assured, how I feel about you has bypassed mere friendship. In fact, I—"

"Lord and Lady Newcastle," Mr. Thomas called out from around the corner ahead. "Come quickly! It is Lord Somerset!"

Lord Somerset? By the look on his butler's face, he could tell things were truly dire.

"Go get Jacob lest I need his help," Charles urged Grace and raced after Thomas.

When he arrived in the great hall, he found Abby in hysterics, and Lord Somerset red in the face, with his mouth agape.

"Was he eating something?" He ordered Thomas to fetch the doctor right away. "Could he be choking?"

"No, he barely managed a sip of tea this morning." Abby shook her head and wrung her hands as Blake and Maude flew downstairs. "What is the matter with him?"

"I do not know." He had never seen this in battle, so he did all he could to make Somerset more comfortable. First, he removed his cravat and unbuttoned his waistcoat, hoping he might breathe easier. Then, rather than waste time getting him to the bedroom, he scooped him out of his gouty chair and laid him on the carpet, praying the change of position might help.

Yet he knew it was too late the moment he laid Reginald's head back. The color had drained from his face, and his eyes were as unseeing as the many soldiers he had watched die.

"Rest in peace, old chap," he said softly, closing Reginald's eyes. Fighting the emotions invoked by seeing death again, he hung his head for a moment and gathered himself before he gave Maude and now Grace and Prudence a look that they needed to be there for their sister.

"I am so sorry, my lady," he said to Abby, "but I fear Lord Somerset is no longer with us."

"Oh, dear Lord." Abby shook her head in denial and stared wide-eyed at Somerset's body. "It cannot be."

Then she released a broken sob. Her sisters ushered her into the drawing room and closed the door behind them. Meanwhile, he carried Somerset to his bed so Abby might eventually say farewell to him in a more dignified location.

"Let me know when the doctor arrives so that I can ensure he sees Lord Somerset well-presented for Lady Somerset," he said to Bessie after covering Reginald with a blanket. "He is not just a peer, but family."

He did not wait for a response but headed for his study, poured a dram of whisky with shaky hands, and downed it, bedamned the hour.

"Are you all right, friend?" Blake asked as he and Jacob joined him. "That was a lot." Then, having clearly been filled in on what he missed, he hesitated a moment before continuing. "As was what happened beforehand."

Fighting frustration at his friends for asking him to lie to Grace, not to mention warfare flashbacks invoked by Reginald's death, he downed another glass of whisky before setting aside the bottle and answering.

"I have been better." He sat behind his desk and sighed. "And I would prefer to be alone right now."

"You might prefer it." Jacob sat in one of the chairs across from him. "But you will not get it." He shook his head. "Not until we are confident you are truly well."

They had seen his fits of melancholy and rage firsthand, so he could not fault them. He would do the same if he were in their shoes. Still, he was angry and said as much. Angry Reginald had lost his life so abruptly under his roof. Even more furious that he had ever agreed to withhold such vital information from Grace.

"Mostly, I am angry at myself, though," he admitted. "Everything Grace said outside is true." He shook his head. "Now I fear I have lost what we found, and I cannot…" Struggling to push past heartache, he tried to put words to it. "I cannot imagine losing any of it. Even one little piece of what she has given me."

"Then tell her that." Blake sat beside Jacob. "Tell her how much you have come to love her because I suspect you have not yet."

"Do you not see?" He frowned. "Even if I did, how could she ever believe me now? Everything we have achieved thus far was because we promised to be honest with one another, yet I was not. No more honest than I imagine her late husband was when he gambled away their fortune." He cursed at the enormity of it. At how clearly he saw things now. "Whether she realizes it or not, I suspect her biggest fear in a relationship is deceit."

"Yours was not so much deceit but ommis—"

"Damn it, man, it *was* deceit, and you know it." He pounded his fist on his desk once and scowled at Jacob. "Deceit when I promised her only transparency and truth."

"Then you need to find a way to make it up to her," Blake said gently. "Because there is a way. I am certain of it."

"I agree," Jacob said. "There has to be a way to…"

He trailed off when a knock came at the door. It was Bessie announcing that the doctor, who was just down the road, had already arrived.

"Very good."

Glad to be free of the conversation, he headed for the door, only to discover taking care of Lord Somerset would prove a much greater ordeal than he imagined.

An ordeal that would take Grace farther away from him than she already was.

Chapter Thirteen

"YOU HAVE TO talk to Lord Newcastle again at some point," Catlin said as she combed Grace's hair. "Perhaps on the carriage ride to Lady Somerset's estate?"

"I have spoken with him." Long enough to thank him for trying to save Reginald and then seeing him well-cared for afterward. "And I will not be riding in Charles' carriage, but my sister's, so I might lend her comfort."

She had assured Charles his presence was not required on the commute nor at the funeral, but he would hear none of it. Not only was Reginald his brother by marriage, but he would be there for her if she needed him. To which she replied that he should rest assured she would not.

Rather, she preferred he not be around.

When she had awoken in his arms yesterday morning, it had been glorious until the fear she had experienced the night before reared its ugly head. What if she somehow let him down when it came to his post-war melancholy? She had seen but a flash of it in his gaze when she wanted to see his chest and wounded eye, so she knew it was very real. A deeply entrenched beast she feared she would not be able to tame.

Unable to sleep and needing time alone to gather her thoughts, she had gone downstairs under the pretense of checking on Alexander, only to find Abby and Reginald already awake.

After that, she'd learned the damning truth.

As it turned out, the way she had felt about William's gambling addiction and the lies he'd told to cover it paled in comparison to learning Charles was every bit as insincere. Worse yet, now she no longer trusted him and could only question how he truly felt about her.

And it was devastating.

It felt as if every moment they shared was false. A show he had put on so he could win over Blake's business. More sadly, still, she had no idea how she would ever be able to tell when he was truthful in the future because of his lack of honesty from the start. As far as she knew, his actions were just lie upon lie, and it broke her heart.

He had broken her heart.

"Then you must speak with Lord Newcastle when you arrive at Lady Abigail's estate," Catlin said, pulling her back to the present. At some point, her friend had crouched in front of her and wiped away another of Grace's tears. "You feel too strongly about each other not to figure this out."

"He only *seems* to feel strongly." Because truly, there was no way to know anything when it came to him. Unable to see beyond her pain, she shook her head. "No, I am sorry. I have no desire to speak with him beyond being civil for Alexander's sake." She glanced at her armoire. "You did pack enough for an extended visit at Abby's, yes?"

"Of course." Catlin appeared troubled. "Though I wish you would reconsider. Perhaps stay on with your sister a few weeks, then return if for no other reason than Alexander's stability? He is newly moved in here, after all."

"Such stability can be found at Abby's," she assured. "With you and Hew there, he will keep up with his studies as I see my younger sister through the first few months of her grieving period."

"Do you not want to be here when the furnishings you and

Lord Newcastle ordered arrive?" Catlin asked softly, cupping Grace's cheek. "The Christmas holiday will be upon us soon, too. Might it not be lovely to bring this castle back to life with new memories?"

"And leave my dear sister alone during such a time?" She frowned. "Absolutely not." It hurt to say it when she had looked forward to putting her own touch on this castle at the holidays, but what choice did she have? "Memories here can wait."

"As you wish," Catlin murmured before she resumed preparing Grace for travel.

Sadly, it was *not* as she wished. None of this was. But what choice did she have? She was sure Abby would need her and Charles would not. Simple as that. Alexander would be fine with Catlin and Hew along.

That in mind, she got into Abby's carriage a short time later, along with Prudence and Maude, to travel alongside the carriage carrying Lord Somerset's body to his final resting place. Alexander would travel with Charles and his uncles. Because it was a lengthy journey, they would stop at an inn halfway there and rest for the night as Reginald continued his trek home to be prepared for burial.

"How are you, Grace?" Maude asked softly, several hours into the trip. Abby and Prudence had dozed off with their heads resting against each other's.

"Sad for Abby," she said just as softly. "What a horrible thing."

"Indeed." Maude gave her a look. "Yet we both know that is not to what I refer."

The previous night, after Abby had gone to bed, she had argued with Prudence and Maude, so they knew how upset she was with them. Both had claimed only to care for her well-being, but she had not walked away feeling satisfied or necessarily cared about. Instead, she'd thought their concern overbearing and uncalled for. And no matter how much they claimed Charles had fought them on it from the start, she had trouble believing them or forgiving him.

Yet that did not stop her from following up with Blake after Charles had tried to save Reginald. Losing the viscount had clearly troubled her husband deeply. Would it trigger war memories? Was he all right? Because she *had* said she would be there for him if he needed her. She'd promised him such but, unlike him, she was intent on maintaining her integrity. Blake had assured her that Charles was well, then addressed what he'd kept from her, defending his friend as passionately as her sisters had.

"He did not like my proposal, Grace." He had shaken his head. "Not one bit. In fact, he said 'no' to it. Refused the idea of you not having your facts up front. If you are going to be upset, I beg of you, be angry with us, not him. He has only ever cared for your well-being. Only ever loved you."

"Love?" She could only be taken aback despite her heart leaping in her chest that he might feel that strongly. "So, he lies to those he *loves*?"

Suffice it to say, it was a losing argument for Lord MacLauchlin, and nothing more came of it than her deciding it best she and Charles took time apart after the funeral until cooler heads prevailed.

Plus, she wanted to be there for Abby. While she knew it had not been a love match between her sister and Lord Somerset, Abby still ached. Not only was Reginald her husband, but she had taken on a caregiver role with him over the past few years. A unique bond unto itself.

"Grace?" Maude said, pulling her back to the here and now when she took her hand. "Besides being mad at me and Prudence, how are you truly?"

"Tired, if I were to be honest." She freed her hand, rested her head back, and closed her eyes. "That said, I would like to rest."

She thought Maude would keep chattering, but she did not, and the remainder of the ride was uneventful. As was the eve at an inn that was so booked up, their servants had to sleep in the carriages. Even worse, she and Alexander were forced to share a room with Charles.

"You two take the bed." Charles gestured at the chair. "I will sleep there."

They had said little at supper, but then the tavern that made up part of the inn was overcrowded and noisy. Not that she had much to say, anyway. By the time she and Alexander lay down, the tension between her and Charles was thicker than ever. It was as though no words existed to mend the distance already growing between them.

She woke several times during the night only to find him not sleeping but staring moodily at the fire with his arms crossed over his chest. At another juncture, he was adding wood to the flames. When she woke in the morning, it was to discover Catlin and Hew sleeping under a blanket on the floor in front of said flames and Charles nowhere to be found.

Almost as if Catlin sensed she had awoken, her maid opened her eyes and looked her way. "Is all well, my lady?"

"It is." She shook her head in confusion. "What happened?"

Catlin yawned and sat up. "The temperature dropped more than anticipated last night, so Lord Newcastle insisted we come in and get warm."

"And where is Lord Newcastle now?"

"Likely below stairs with the other servants." She nudged Hew awake. "If I understood correctly, he meant to see them resting and warm in front of the tavern fire."

"I see." However upset she might be with him, she was not surprised Charles was, at least, thoughtful of his servants and concerned with the welfare of others. She was thankful for it, too, and said as much to him after she and the others made their way downstairs for a bite before they set out again.

He offered no response other than a brisk nod, but then it seemed he was as out of sorts as she. His eye was red rimmed from lack of sleep, and day-old stubble lined his jaw.

"What a kind thing Charles did for the servants," Abby said later that morning as they continued their journey toward

Somerset. Her sister had been gazing out the window sadly before issuing the compliment out of nowhere. "But not surprising given what he did for my dear husband." She looked Grace's way. "I most appreciate all of it. From him trying to save Reginald's life to the presentation he insisted be made...postpartum for my benefit. He is caring, indeed."

"You already said as much, and I passed on the message to him," she said gently, worried about her sister. Abby might be more adventurous and vivacious than most, but she also suffered from an overly soft heart. One that Grace was right to assume would hurt most unexpectedly when Reginald passed. It would not be broken but perhaps flailing. Lonely and without purpose.

It was seen so clearly after the funeral when she sank into a melancholy that made Grace relieved she had decided to remain behind. That someone would be here for these first few months.

"Are you sure you do not want me to stay?" Charles asked after insisting they take a few moments alone before he returned home. Although reluctant, she had agreed to join him in the gardens behind Abby's townhome. "It is clear your sister is going through a period of adjustment, and you could use the help getting her affairs in order as she begins her mourning period."

"No, you should return to your castle and see to things." She had no clue what those *things* were and, honestly, had no interest in knowing. "Meanwhile, as I am sure you understand, I think it best Alexander remain here with me. Mr. Hew will continue seeing to his studies, of course."

"Of course," he said softly. Charles hesitated a moment, clearly grappling with what he wanted to say before he once again repeated what he had already said. "You cannot know how sorry I am." He looked at her with what some might perceive as his heart in his eyes. "I never meant to hurt you. Please talk to me, Grace."

"I have been talking to you."

"Not really." He shook his head. "Not like we did before."

"And I might never again." She arched her eyebrows when he

seemed disgruntled by that. "Why should that surprise you when the way we talked was supposed to have been honest and without preamble? Something you surely understand is remiss now." She shook her head. "Something we may never get back."

"Then might we start anew?" he said. "Because I can think of no one else I would rather do so with again and again until you trust me once more. Until you understand how much I care for you."

She could not help but notice he did not use the word 'love'. Despite how upset she remained with him, she was surprised how that made her chest tighten with emotion. How much it hurt her on top of everything else.

"And how do you imagine we might start anew?"

"By addressing a concern, I should have realized you suffered at the very beginning," he said bluntly. "My negligence of funds during my grieving period. One that went on for far too long and caused others to suffer. Negligence you have every right to be wary of after William's mismanagement of your estate."

She started to shake her head that she had not meant to say such in the heat of the moment, but he went on.

"As you know, I have already rid my companies of poor management," Charles said. "When I return home, I intend to take control and see things returned to how they once were." He shook his head. "Not because of Blake's incoming business either, but because I truly want to. Because I care again for the first time in longer than I can remember." His voice dropped an octave. "I want to see you and Alexander taken care of. See after his health going forward. Make sure he has the education he deserves. And I want you out from under the constant worry that he might not."

While tempted to respond, she found her throat thick with emotion that he might mean it. So, she gave herself a moment to gather her feelings before responding. More pointedly, she refused to be the soft-hearted fool everyone had thought she was with William.

"While I appreciate your goals, my lord—" she kept things

impersonal—"I am sure you understand, words are just words for now." She shook her head once. "Nothing more and nothing less."

"I do understand," he said. "And intend to show you they can be more, indeed. That they can be put into action and become reality." He kissed the back of her hand like he had when they were courting. His gaze lingered on her face. "You will see, Grace. I will prove myself to you. Prove that I am nothing like William."

Caught off guard by that, she blinked at him. "What do you know of William and me?" Then, growing angry and perhaps a tad embarrassed, she shook her head again. "You know nothing of us. Nothing of how it was between us."

"Because you have not told me." He did not shy away at her building frustration. "Nor have I told you of my time with Charlotte when I should have much sooner. How losing her and my child felt. I should have shared everything right from the start. Right from the beginning and without pause when I realized how much I wanted you. Wanted you from nearly the moment I laid eyes on you."

"Yet you did not share," she said softly. "Any more than I."

"But I will." He kissed her hand again, this time with closed eyes and lingering lips as if cherishing the act before he looked at her again. "I will write you and share everything so we might start anew. We will take all the time you need and make this right because nothing is worth more." He shook his head. "Nothing at all."

She never got a chance to respond before dinner was served. Thank goodness, too, because she did not know how to react. How could written words make a difference at this juncture? To her mind, the best way to move forward after she stayed with Abby for a few months was to revert to a version of what she and Charles had first agreed to. She told him as much, too, before he departed.

"I cannot see us resuming our friendship, but perhaps a civil partnership as we move forward," she said. "Not just for our sakes but for Alexander's. I know you care for him, and he needs that in his life. That said, write as often as you like, but I cannot promise I will respond."

"Understood." He kissed her cheek, then looked at her with unmistakable determination. "Here is to a civil partnership, at the very least."

As it happened, he meant that.

So said what she received from him soon thereafter.

Chapter Fourteen

CHARLES COULD ADMIT he had hoped he and Grace might make more headway before he returned home but understood why she remained hesitant and did not blame her in the least. So, rather than drown in grief or let his mind grow dark with war memories, he focused on being what Grace deserved.

Moreover, what he had owed himself for a long time.

Not a man full of grief and self-pity, but the productive businessman he had been before he lost Charlotte and their child. So as soon as he got home, he embarked on a journey to resurrect his life.

What struck him as most interesting was he managed it without Grace. Better still, he found it easier without her there. It allowed him to see things more clearly. How broken he had been. How she could never have fixed him had their relationship flourished.

Only he could fix him.

To that end, he went to work quite literally. First, he finally stepped foot on a boat again to oversee his various businesses. Faced a part of his past he had let rule him for far too long. Then he hired more responsible management as well as additional staff for their estate.

All of which he shared with Grace via letters.

Dearest Grace,

I hope that you, Alexander, and Lady Abigail are faring well. While I work toward reestablishing my businesses, I thought to keep you updated on our home renovations, not just with words but with images. Therefore, I hired an artist to capture different changes, so you feel part of everything here while still lending comfort to your sister. The first image is included. I am sure you will understand.

Your Husband,
Charles

He enclosed an image of the life-sized portrait of his ancestor and Longshank's right-hand man banished to the attic rather than hanging downstairs.

After that, he continued writing her daily, hoping for a reply but determined not to get upset if none came. Instead, he hired workers to fix the castle, sure to send both her and Alexander letters tracking their progress. The boy, especially, as he would appreciate the history and reconstruction of specific areas.

He saved the best news for Grace, though.

My Lovely Grace,

I am pleased to report that the castle was built well and will only need simple renovations, after all. Truth be told, I thought the report on its health would be far worse, but it seems our estate is determined to persevere every bit as much as I hope we will.

Yours Always,
Charles

He included images of the various renovations, then sent several more letters about ongoing renovations, despite no reply. She wanted more like he had promised. He knew it like he knew how to breathe. But where to start? Something he asked Mrs. Bessie when she flitted around him in front of the fire one night.

She was forever worried he might sink into one of his states and checked in far too frequently.

"How does one fix this, my friend?" he wondered absently, sipping his tea. He had avoided alcohol since returning, lest it lend an extra layer of darkness to any potential melancholy. "I promised Grace I would tell her everything, yet I cannot seem to get beyond business and renovations." He perked an eyebrow at her. "Perhaps that is all that is required?"

"Most certainly not, if you promised Lady Newcastle everything." Bessie replaced cooled tea with hot and frowned at him. "Though I suppose I must understand what everything means?"

"It means Charlotte..." he said softly. "And all she entails."

Bessie thought about that a moment before she gestured at the chair beside him. "Might I sit?"

"Need you ask?"

"I suppose not, but you know I am trying to act proper and such." She sank into the chair and considered him. "Now I must ask, do you want the easy or difficult answer?"

He quirked the corner of his mouth. "As if you are not in the habit of giving me the most difficult one, to keep me in line."

"Quite right." Bessie thought about it. "If I were honest, I would recommend more personal letters than you have sent thus far." She wagged her finger back and forth. "Not too intimate, mind you. She is not looking for romance but who you were before you met. The man who loved Charlotte. His unborn child. Who eventually lost himself to war."

Before he could respond, Bessie went on.

"And I would keep your artist on target, too." Bessie gestured at their surroundings. "All of this is one thing." More serious than ever, she pressed her hand to her chest. "This, the heart beating in your chest, is another. Grace needs to truly hear it. See it. Become part of you in a way you have not yet allowed her."

Understanding her meaning, he shook his head. "I do not know that I can. Not...all of it."

"Yet all of it she must hear," Bessie said softly. "And you

know it. Have known it since the moment you fell in love with her."

Bessie did not say precisely when she thought that had happened, but she stood then, kissed his cheek, and left him to his thoughts. More so, she left paper and a quill at his side so he might seize the moment to write the first letter that really mattered.

How to phrase such, though? How to tell her things that were all his and Charlotte's?

At the very beginning, he supposed.

Dearest Grace,

I have said much so far but nothing at all. Perhaps because some part of me would not have anyone outside my castle knowing the dynamics of the love that developed between Charlotte and me. Developed, you might ask? What a strange word to describe love. But it would be the right one, as ours was an arranged marriage between our families.

You see, while beautiful and much sought after, Charlotte was troubled, for lack of a better way to put it. Prone to fits of hysteria that none understood, her kin felt her something that needed to be dealt with. Yet, despite her unrest, she also needed to be married off well. I, in turn, required a wife, so we were married, hardly knowing one another. Or should I say, barely knowing each other, beyond childhood memories?

He went to keep writing but found it too difficult, so he ended the letter, promising more to come. Then, however difficult, he had his artist pen a picture of him and Charlotte as children to include in the letter.

While tempted to wait for a response from Grace if, in fact, it ever came, he found he could not hold back, so a few days later, started writing again. Told her all of it. Things no one outside his household knew.

My Dearest Grace,

While I grew stubborn the moment I sent off my last letter and vowed I would not write again until I heard from you, I find…"

What *did* he find? He thought about it. What was it he felt exactly? *Her*, he realized. Not Charlotte but Grace. Not just in a romantic sense but in a way that seemed part of him. Vital and necessary. So, he kept writing. Let her into his previous marriage. The damage that had been done to his heart, no matter how fiercely he had come to love his late wife.

"I find I need to tell you that Charlotte did not return my love."

He stared at the words for several moments and started to crumble the letter in denial but froze. Not because he wanted to soften Grace by sending it regardless but because it was the first time he had acknowledged the truth, let alone written it down.

Yet now he had.

This was a first step.

What now, though? How to share something so incredibly personal? *One word at a time*, he supposed. One word after the other, no matter how hard, if it brought him closer to Grace and helped her understand.

So, he kept writing.

I have no doubt that Charlotte liked me, but as to love, I remain unsure as she was often difficult to understand. Sometimes full of life. Other times like a wildflower trapped in the shade. During those darker hours, I often found her perched on a cliff's edge as if ready to jump, but she never did.

Rather, she made a game out of my fear that she might do something horrible. For example, she offered me flowers that only grew on our more treacherous cliff paths so I might know how endangered she had been. Not to frighten or hurt me, I do not think, but to let me know she could never truly be mine. Not entirely. She was too fragile. Incapable of ever committing fully to anyone.

He hovered with his quill over the paper and hung his head. Remembered all too well what it had felt like to realize that. To know his dear childhood friend was challenged, for lack of a better word. That she would never be normal, no matter how hard he tried to bring her back from the precipice of her troubled mind.

She had oftentimes been somewhere else and always would be.

Leaving the letter off at that point for now, he sealed it, but not before adding the dried and flattened remnants of flowers Charlotte had picked for him. He had held on to them for too long as it was. Now might they speak words from the beyond the grave, if only he understood what those words were.

His conversations with Charlotte had gone from making sense to no sense at all, then back to being sensible again. Enough to let him know she would never fully be with him. Never be anywhere fully, for that matter, which only made him try harder and care more because her family predictably abandoned her after they married.

"As you know, she is quite fine on occasion," Mr. Thomas had assured him one night when Charlotte flung everything to the floor, from antique vases to priceless dinnerware. "Just give her a moment to find herself again, yes?"

"Of course," he had assured his distraught butler. "Always."

"And I meant that," he continued in his following letter to Grace. "Because the fact of the matter was, I had become quite enamored with Charlotte as a boy. She had defended me in a brawl as though Queen Elizabeth leading England into battle and...well...I saw how much she cared then. Not for friendship, per se, but for defending those who were teased. For those whom she considered unable to defend themselves. A true warrioress, to be sure."

Remembering how ferocious little Charlotte had been, he smiled and continued.

So, as I am sure you understand, I felt the need to do the same for her years later when we were married. I was determined to truly know her when so few could be bothered. And I was never so thankful I did. Never so grateful that I sat her down and spoke with her. Saw past the mania in her eyes, as they called it, to the calm within.

And there was calm.

Calmer than I suspect anyone realized. A peace to be found in her turbulent soul. A happiness so extraordinary I admit I became addicted. Wanted that buoyant joy with me always. Strove to bring it back even when crushing melancholy inevitably overtook her for days before she once again became a woman who enchanted all.

I will share more soon. Until then, wishing you and Alexander all the best.

Yours,
Charles

With that letter, he included an image of Charlotte at her saddest and one at her happiest. Two pictures that did not seem to be the same woman. But then she had not been. Not at all.

Yet still, I loved her deeply and was never happier than when she became pregnant. Unfortunately, I could not say the same for Charlotte. Where before, she had had good days and bad, I am afraid they all became bad after she was with child. Once she got through the sickness that often comes with the first few months of pregnancy, she fell into either a melancholy that had her crying for days or a madness of sorts that is hard to describe.

Yet describe he would no matter how difficult.

Sadly, she did not want the child from the moment of con-

ception. Swore that it would take her life. If that were not enough, despite agreeing we wanted a child, she grew paranoid and claimed her eventual death had been my intention all along.

He paused again, rallied his emotions, and tried not to reflect on those excruciating months.

While Charlotte's were the rantings of what some might call a madwoman, sadly enough, her fears came to pass in childbirth. I cannot tell you the heartache of burying your wife and child. The unspeakable pain. An endless ache I tried to escape by enlisting. Yet even in battle, thoughts of them were with me. Her cries became those of the soldiers I fought alongside. Who died beside me. A suffering that filled every part of me. Consumed me. Made it hard to care about anything anymore.

Rather than focus on his injuries, he recalled those first months after returning home.

After returning from war, I went to a very dark place that made it impossible to see what was happening around me. From the state of my castle to the health of my businesses. None of it mattered because it no longer existed. My thoughts only had room for anger and bitterness. Self-hatred. Truth be known, I did not realize how far I had sunken until I met you.

Until something came to life in me, I never thought I would feel again.

He paused again and thought about how to phrase what he wanted to say, as there seemed no words to describe it. Or perhaps there were not enough words.

When I met you, I started to see what I had allowed my life to become. How lost I truly was. The kind of man I had turned into. I cannot tell you how much I wish I had seen the damage happening to my businesses. Not just for the sake of my heir-

looms but for the servants who lost employment and those who remained. It was unfair to them all.

Meeting you made me see everything more clearly, and I confess I was embarrassed. Ashamed of what I had let happen to my finances. To the people I cared about. They did not deserve it any more than you deserved being lied to.

Because it was a lie the moment I did not tell you everything.

I can only say that when my friends finally convinced me to keep the truth from you, your and Alexander's wellbeing was all that mattered. The most important thing to me. The idea that you might have ended up with someone with ill intentions was unbearable. I suppose, to my way of thinking at the time, the risk outweighed an even greater risk.

How could it not when I had already fallen in love with you?

Because I do love you, Grace. More than I thought possible. And I will continue to show you how much until you finally believe me. Not just that, but I am determined to earn back your trust if it is the last thing I do.

He could only hope this letter helped and that she might finally write back to him.

More so, that she would decide to come home sooner rather than later.

Chapter Fifteen

"WOULD THAT BE another missive from your loving husband, dear sister?" Abby mused when her butler held out a silver tray with a letter for Grace. "You must have quite the collection by now."

They sat in Abby's drawing room, enjoying a game of cribbage. The holiday had come and gone, and her sister appeared to be doing better.

"Quite the collection, indeed." Grace took the letter and thanked Abby's butler before she sighed and stared at the seal. "I must admit, he is as relentless as he said he would be."

"And for that, I applaud him." Abby arched her brows. "Have you written him back yet?"

"I started to." How could she not after one of his more recent letters? After sharing what he had about Charlotte, then declaring how much he had come to love Grace? "But I admit, I struggle to find the right words."

"Likely because you have been in denial of them for so long," Abby said bluntly. "So I suspect, setting aside that Charles more than deserves to hear from you at this point, writing down your feelings about your previous marriage will prove helpful."

"Or anger me." She laid down her cards.

"Which is all part of the process, I am afraid." Abby laid down her cards as well and counted their points before shuffling. "How do you think Charles felt when writing you about his wife? About what he had let his businesses come to? His estate? That could not have been easy and likely opened up old wounds. But he did it regardless, in order that you might better understand him. So you might give him another chance."

She and Abby were close, and she knew her sister would never repeat anything, so she had shared quite a bit about the contents of Charles' letters. Felt the need to talk to someone about how they made her feel, which, honestly, was remarkably sad for him. It seemed both of their spouses had worn two faces on some level. Had possessed dual spirits within one body.

"He *has* been remarkably forthright." She sipped her tea and thought about the letter that came soon after the one about Charlotte. Charles had focused more on *their*—not *his*—businesses' progress. He even went so far as to include some ledgers redacted enough to be discreet in case his correspondence ended up in someone else's hands.

> *When you return home, you may look over everything in full. Something I insist you often do, not only so you understand the trade but so you might see where our money is going and coming from. Not just because I feel it your right but because I want you to have the peace of mind knowing the state of our finances will bring you.*

"He *has* been forthright, and you owe him the same in return." Abby gave Grace a knowing look. "And I am not just referring to your former marriage but to the secret you think I have not figured out yet."

"How did you know?" she asked softly, often amazed at how perceptive Abby could be.

"Ah, so I was right." Abby smiled in delight. "You *are* with child again. I thought you might be when you decided to stay longer than three months. If that were not enough, you have the same glow about you that you had carrying Alexander."

"I glow?" As outlandish as it sounded, somehow, that did not surprise her. She did not suffer sickness like some women but instead felt overly-healthy, perhaps because of sheer happiness. A feeling of joy she had felt with Alexander, and now, whether she and Charles were at their best or not, she felt just as strongly about this child.

"Oh, you most certainly glow," Abby gushed, clearly glad Grace's secret was finally out in the open. "And you continually wear this soft little smile like you have already dreamt of your unborn babe and cannot wait to meet him or her."

She touched her mouth absently. "Do I?"

"Most certainly."

"Who knew?" she murmured.

"I did." Abby kept grinning like a child with a treat before she grew rather serious. "And while I shall miss you dearly when you go, I feel it high time you write that letter and then make your way back home."

She could admit the thought held far more appeal now than before. Not just because of how much Charles had shared with her but because she missed him. He had become someone she enjoyed spending time with and talking to. Admittedly, the only thing holding her back was Abby and perhaps even her own pregnancy. What would he make of it? Given what he had gone through with Charlotte, would he be happy or terrified?

"I cannot leave you quite yet, Abby," she said. "It has not been enough time."

"It has been more than enough time." Rather than finish the game, Abby waved her off and put away the cribbage board and cards. "I still miss Reginald, but as you can plainly see, my mood has improved. That said, even though I am still mourning, it is time to be among my friends again."

She frowned. "Am I not your friend?"

"One of my very best." Abby set several sheets of paper, a quill, and a jar of ink in front of Grace. "Even so, you have a husband who misses you and a son who, not surprisingly considering the endless letters Charles has written him, misses his new father very much. Thus, like me, as I work toward leaving the past behind and focusing on the future by penning my friends, so too shall you by writing about your previous marriage, then going home to your current one."

Abby was about to flounce off, but Grace caught her hand and looked at her most seriously. "While I know it is high time I share more with Charles about my previous marriage, do you think I should tell him about the child I lost before Alexander? Would that serve any purpose at this point or only lend to Charles' fear that I could very well lose another?"

"That must be up to you, darling sister." Abby squeezed her hand and thought about it. "Though I would be inclined to think if you wanted him to keep no secrets from you, then you must be prepared to offer the same in return." She cocked her head and considered Grace. "That is if you truly only ever want honesty in your new marriage."

Before she could respond, Abby swept out of the room, leaving her alone with her thoughts. With what she should and should not say. Which, she realized, must be everything because Abby was right. How could she want complete honesty from Charles if she were not willing to offer the same?

Where to begin, though? With William, naturally. But at what point?

However difficult to narrow down, there were indeed other things to address first. Most pointedly, the more critical parts of her husband's letters.

Dear Charles,

As you can see, it took me some time to reply. Time I needed to see to my sister's welfare and contemplate how you and I might move forward together. While I cannot say with certainty it will be on the path you wish, I must confess your letters have helped me understand you better.

She paused momentarily, wondering if that sounded right, but she could not think of any other way to phrase things.

Whilst I know we promised one another we would not deal in pity, I cannot help but express how sorry I am about the difficult road you traveled with Charlotte.

She thought about the images he had sent of Charlotte as a child and then as an adult. Perhaps she should speak to her beauty, for she had been stunning. Yet that did not seem appropriate nor relevant, given the circumstances. Setting aside loving someone who did not return such affection, it sounded like Charlotte had been quite mad. And while he said he adored her when they were both children, implying he was not opposed to the union, the fact was, it had been arranged.

Therefore, neither was given a choice.

Worse still, it sounded like Charlotte's family knew precisely what he was in for and found him a convenient way to deal with their problem. Not *problem*. She did not like that word to describe his late wife's ailment, for it *was* that. A sickness of the mind that needed the sort of help Charles had been ill-equipped to provide.

I cannot imagine how difficult watching Charlotte suffer must have been for you, other than to say I understand on a much lesser scale. Because even though William's circumstances were markedly different, I know he suffered too. His inability to stop craving gambling dens would sometimes make him dour. Hard to understand. Often impossible with which to communicate. Yet I loved him dearly. Loved him with my whole heart despite everything.

She stopped writing again and stared at her words. Was it right to compare Charlotte and William when Charles' late wife had suffered so much more? When Charles had undoubtedly suffered more than Grace? She blinked back tears and shook her head at the sudden anger and sadness her queries invoked. Emotions that were born of denying for too long just how difficult things had been in her previous marriage.

During our first year, all seemed well. Truly lovely. We

were happy. He was happy. Then again, those were the days before his addiction started getting the better of him. If I'm being honest with myself, I suppose his compulsion to gamble became greater – after we lost our first child. It was very early in my pregnancy but still devastating. Incredibly heartbreaking.

Yet she had been lucky enough to have another. She blinked back tears and went on.

A little under a year later, I became pregnant again, and Alexander was born. He was three when William's gambling intensified. While inclined to say it was because Alexander started having breathing problems around that time, and William wanted us more financially secure for medical reasons, I now see that was only my excuse for his behavior and wishful thinking on my part.

She hesitated and dabbed at more tears, grateful for the fresh handkerchief her sister had conveniently, and no doubt intentionally, left behind. Because once she started sharing her feelings, her tears seemed endless.

I initially thought William might be having an affair because he was staying out all night, but it wasn't long before the gossip started about how often he was seen in the gambling dens. That, in turn, made me pay closer attention to his gaming at gatherings.

She inhaled a ragged breath before she went on.

I would like to tell you I saw it then and knew right away he had a problem. But the better way to say it, the truthful way, is to confess that when I did see it, I denied it. Convinced myself it was my imagination. Why, you ask? Quite simple. I could not fathom him putting his family at such risk. Alexander at such risk. So, over the next few years, I denied and denied, then denied it some more.

Once again, she paused with pen over paper when she nearly lied.

> *If I were to be honest, I denied it until the very end because it hurt too much. I blamed William pushing me away during his losing streaks on his lack of sleep. Naturally, pulling me close when he won was proof that he never had a problem to begin with. Only after he passed and I learned how poorly off he had left us did I realize the extent of his sickness, as it were. Even worse, the depth to which I had fooled myself. How could I have done that when I was supposed to be looking out for Alexander? I am his mother. The one who is supposed to ensure his safety at all costs.*
>
> *So how could I have let William hurt us so very much? Hurt our son so much?*

Until she put it into words, she had not realized just how much blame she had put on herself, instead of placing it solely on William. Regardless, she knew now that she did, in fact, shoulder some of the blame not for William's addiction, never that, but for how she had handled it. She should have spoken up more often and been firmer in her stance the few times she did. She should have been a fierce advocate for Alexander's financial future.

Her *own* future.

She removed her wedding band and blinked at its inscription through tears. Emotions she had long denied herself. *To Friendship and All it Entails*

Friendship was not something she and William had ever worried about, and she wondered, no *knew*, that they should have. It might have made all the difference if they had focused on such from the start. May have given her the courage to stand up to him like she had Charles. To say what needed saying and act in Alexander's best interest. Because, whether William was at the root of all their problems or not, she had chosen not to acknowledge her late husband's troubling behavior in its entirety.

She pressed her lips against her ring before sliding it back onto her finger and picking up the quill again.

As angry as I am at William and myself, I am not so foolish to think things would have been easier had I confronted him more forcibly. He was my husband, so no matter what, I would have had to stand by his side and hope he changed his ways. Prayed he put Alexander first. While some might argue he gambled in hopes of gaining wealth for our family, it is safe to say it was more for the thrill it offered him.

Certainly not to leave his family better off.

I believe if anyone other than me truly wishes Alexander a bright future, it is you, Charles. While I remain dismayed that you were not truthful with me from the beginning, I can better understand why you were not after reading your letters. I also recognize my anger at you was not only because of your dishonesty but because I feared being lied to again by my spouse.

That I would fall right back into my own bad habits.

Yet I did not, any more than you are like William. I see that clearly now, so given Abby is on the mend, Alexander and I will return home. I know he misses you terribly, so I return with no hesitation that you will only ever put his needs above your own.

Your Friend,
Grace

While tempted to sign her letter with a personal endearment, she held back for now. She believed Charles did love her and suspected he knew she felt the same, but when she finally said it, better that it be in person. She rested her hand on her womb, wanting it to be after all truths had been revealed between them.

So, within a few days of sending the letter, confident Abby would be all right, she and the others readied themselves for the long journey northeast. Her sister shed happy tears as she embraced her, then held her at arm's length. "I will miss you, but I am so glad you and Alexander are returning to Charles. I suspect he would have wanted you to wait so he could escort you, but I understand your need to rush home now you realize that is where you belong." Her gaze flickered from Grace's stomach back to her face. "Where all of you belong."

Outside of Catlin, only Abby knew thus far, so she appreciated her sister's discretion.

"I am confident you will be safe with the men I hired to escort you," Abby went on. "Even so, I expect a letter the moment you arrive, letting me know all is well."

Grace glanced at the sturdy-looking men who would be riding alongside their carriage as though they traveled in a more perilous time.

"I will write you straight away," she assured her sister. "I expect to hear from you often and hope you will consider visiting soon."

Abby's gaze flickered to her belly once more, and she grinned. "You may count on it, dear sister."

Little more was said after that, and they started on their way.

To be expected, Alexander was excited. He had changed considerably over these past few months of corresponding with Charles. Reverted back to his old self. Better still, he seemed happier than before his father died.

Granted, there had been a brief period of change while William fought an illness that took him quickly, but looking back, Alexander had begun changing beforehand. Something she had likely not wanted to see any more than she wanted to believe William's addiction was so severe.

Now, she could say with utmost confidence that Alexander's happiness was genuine. As authentic as his sadness had been when Charles returned north for business months ago. Yet her new husband had written her son as often as he had penned her, involving him in every aspect of the castle's renovations.

Charles' inclusivity had paid off, too, because Alexander was bursting with anticipation.

His breathing episodes were a tad more frequent at Abby's, yet he still seemed happier despite them, which had everything to do with Charles. He had kept him in good spirits by making him feel included in everything and by being not just an admirable father figure but a good friend.

"Did you see the latest, Mother?" Alexander presented the most recent images Charles had sent. He pointed to the right of a bookshelf and tried at a wink. "While Captain Charles did not say it in so many words, I believe there is a hidden entrance to a tunnel somewhere around here." Sure to be most secretive about it, he tucked the image away as quickly as he had whipped it out. "I will speak to him about it when we arrive home. Moreover, we will discuss me finally discovering our castle's secrets." He nodded once, quite serious. "Those meant for its masters alone, of course."

"Be that as it may," she made clear, trying not to worry that the stale, dusty air might be too much for him, "I am our castle's mistress, so know, Young Master, that I shall be with you every step of the way."

Alexander offered no response, but she knew he understood there would be no way around that stipulation. She could only hope Charles' idea of wrapping breathable cloth over Alexander's nose and mouth was helpful. To that end, they practiced with a handkerchief before settling into a journey that proved pleasant despite the time of year. As did their overnight stay at an inn and their trek northward the next day.

All continued to go well, and everyone grew excited when Charles' castle arose in the distance. She'd had no idea how much she missed this place until she saw it on the horizon. Her thoughts returned to the first day they had arrived here with him. The endless raindrops in a carriage that had since been retired. The laughter they had all shared.

She did not doubt such entertaining times would continue to happen often over the years. Like Alexander and perhaps herself, Charles was undergoing a change that meant happier times ahead. Or so she thought until they pulled up in front of the castle, and he greeted her in a most unexpected way.

One very much the opposite of happy.

Chapter Sixteen

THOMAS KNOCKED ON Charles' study door. "My lord?"

"What is it?" He bit back more sharply than intended but worry had him in a foul mood. While he had been elated to receive Grace's letter a few days ago, he was equally dismayed when he learned she and Alexander meant to travel the whole of England without him there to see to their safety.

"What are you *thinking*, Grace?" he had cursed under his breath. "You should have waited for me."

He had promptly readied a horse for travel but realized there were any number of routes her driver might have decided to take given the time of year. What if Charles chose the wrong one and missed them?

"You should wait right here for them, my lord," both Bessie and Thomas had insisted. "They will arrive safely."

So said Abby, whose letter had arrived shortly thereafter informing him she had hired war veterans like him to keep watch over them.

"Does Lady Somerset even know these men?" he had muttered, raking a hand through his hair. "For all we know, they could have taken her coin only to—"

"Get your family home safely." Bessie had looked at him sternly, leaving no room for argument. "I might not have known Lady Somerset all that long, but if I have figured out nothing else about her, it is that none are more precious to her than her sisters and her nephew. So she would have hired trusted men to look after Grace and Alexander." She shook her head. "Your sister by marriage would have spared no expense, my lord."

Be that as it may, he was on edge and had barely slept since he received word they were coming. So naturally, when Thomas informed him one of their own carriages approached, he rushed outside, relieved to see it was, in fact, Grace and Alexander.

"Captain Charles," Alexander exclaimed the moment he was out of the carriage. He tried to exercise good manners but failed when Charles crouched to welcome the boy into his arms for a long-overdue embrace. They held onto each other for a moment before he stood and scowled at Grace when that was the last thing he had envisioned doing when they reunited.

Tempted to both chastise her for being foolish and yank her into his arms, he bowed at the waist quite formally instead. "Welcome back, my lady."

"My lord." Confusion edged her eyebrows together as she curtsied in turn. "Is everything well? You seem troubled."

"No more than any man would be when his family foolishly risks their lives traveling across England without giving me a chance to escort them."

He might be upset but would not take it out on the men who had, in the end, gotten them here safely. He'd not treat fellow veterans poorly. Rather, he thanked them both personally and insisted they stay on. Food and accommodation would be provided, and their horses looked after. Tomorrow, he would offer them full-time positions as Grace and Alexander's private guard for future travel.

"We do live in the nineteenth rather than the fifteenth century, my lord," Grace reminded as they made their way up the stairs. "So, you need not be so upset."

"My name is Charles, so enough with 'my lord'," he grumbled under his breath and sighed. In truth, while he was right about the risks of traveling, Grace was undoubtedly ignorant about how dangerous it could be. "And our current century matters little when it comes to a woman and boy traveling alone with cases full of fine clothing and jewelry." He tried to soften his tone because he did not want to argue. Not now that he knew they were safe. "Surely, you understand, setting aside how vulnerable you are as a woman, that our country is not without desperate poverty-ridden people. Those who would steal anything to put food in their children's bellies.

"And I would not blame them," he went on before she could reply. "For I would likely do the same if I were in their position and needed to care for you and Alexander. Desperate times call for desperate measures as the divide of classes only grows more prevalent. Surely you know that. Surely—"

"I do, Charles," she cut in softly before he could go on. Good thing, too, because he was suddenly in a mood to talk post-war economics and how so many of England's citizens suffered where others enjoyed lavishness beyond their needs.

"And I am sorry we worried you so," Grace continued. "Truly." She urged him to stop and looked at him. Considered him with the sort of sincerity he had missed. "If I must be honest, my only thought was of getting back here to you." She shook her head. "Not because some might say that is a wife's place but because I missed my friend. Our talks. Who you are. Who I am with you." She glanced at the soldiers, who were determined to see to their horses personally despite the stable hands provided. "Trust me when I say I will not do that again." Her gaze returned to his face. "You have my word."

He nearly touched her cheek, pulled her close, and kissed her, but he was unsure where their relationship lay. She had shared a great deal in her letter but did not include any endearments beyond friendship. If anything, she seemed somewhat distant.

Yet she had let him in, and that was all he wanted so they might start anew.

It had been disheartening to learn she'd lost a child too. He wished she had shared such sooner so he could have, at the very least, held her. Soothed her. Related to her as only he could. Because, as it turned out, at least partly, she had been empathetic rather than sympathetic back at the beginning. Very much understood and related to his heartache.

The two said little more as they headed inside and sat down for refreshments. Alexander, however, had a great deal to say, and it seemed Grace was as happy to hear them chat as he was to actually talk with the boy again. Eventually, they retired to prepare for a dinner Charles had made sure included all of Grace and Alexander's favorites.

"How are you, my lord?" Thomas asked while he adjusted Charles' cravat. He eyed him with concern. "You seem quite subdued when you have done little more than rant and rave for the better part of two days."

"And for that, I am sorry, Thomas." He stared into the mirror and saw the worry still etched around his eyes. The furrowed brow he could not seem to lose. "I guess, in some strange way, I suffer now like I did when I first came home from war. Somehow, the thought of harm coming to Alexander and Grace felt like the harm I watched come to many during battle."

"Understood." Thomas adjusted his cravat a bit more and directly met his gaze, much like Bessie would have if she stood here. It seemed his valet saw him teetering on the edge of old demons based on what he said next. "Yet those you watched die during war are, sadly, long gone, and Lady Grace and Master Alexander are right here. More to the point, they need you here too. We all do."

"But of course," he said a little too quickly, rolling his shoulders. "Where else would I be?"

"Elsewhere, my lord." Thomas nodded once that Charles was presentable and stepped back. Yet his friend's gaze never left his face, and his words were never so serious as he spoke in a military fashion in which Charles could better relate. "It was one thing losing Lord Somerset on your watch. Another thing altogether thinking you might lose your family…another family. Because you *do* feel responsible for the one behind you and the one ahead of you, whether you could have controlled either scenario or not."

He supposed his man was right and nodded because he was capable of little more at the moment. Yet he kept Thomas' words in mind when he joined Grace and Alexander at dinner for the first time in nearly four months. The boy was well-presented, and Grace somehow even lovelier than he remembered if such were possible. Aglow in a way that must have been there all along, yet he saw more clearly now because he had missed her so much.

They caught up over creamy chestnut soup, followed by perfectly seasoned flounder served with spinach and potatoes, followed by various sweets.

"I cannot wait to tell you all my thoughts about possible renovations to our already impressive castle, Captain Charles." Alexander chatted away, oblivious to how Charles kept trying to catch Grace's eye with a smile or lingering gaze. "I realize I understand little about such matters, but Aunt Abigail, I mean Lady Somerset, procured me books on old English castle architecture. I, of course, read them from front to back in my spare time, so I believe I might be able to contribute advice to future endeavors."

"I do not doubt you will." Proud of Alexander for taking such initiative, he smiled at the boy, then looked at Grace, as this was ultimately her decision. "I thought if you two are up for it tomorrow, we might finally explore the hidden parts of the castle. Those its family should know." He looked from Grace to Alexander. "From its mistress to its young master."

"Oh, yes, absolutely." Alexander's eyes grew especially bright when he addressed Grace. "If such is all right with Mother, that is." He fought a grin when he glanced from Charles back to her. "I mean to say, this castle's most noteworthy mistress."

"Of course it is." Grace met his barely repressed grin. "I would love to explore the castle's secrets as long as you agree to wear a face covering."

"I do."

"Very good then."

That said, they finished a lovely meal before Catlin saw Alexander to bed.

"Might we enjoy an after-dinner nightcap before you retire?" he asked Grace, assuming she must be tired. "Perhaps take a few moments to tour some rooms so you can finally see the changes made in your absence firsthand?"

He waited with bated breath at the flicker of hesitation in her eyes before she nodded graciously. "I would like that." She glanced at the great hall tentatively. "Perhaps we might start out there as I could not help but notice something quite familiar."

"We can, indeed." He held out his elbow to her. "Come, Lady Newcastle. Allow me to show you both what I wrote about and what I kept a surprise."

"How intriguing." She slipped her arm into his. "So, you did not share everything?"

"I did not." Happy to have his dear friend back more than anything, he winked at her. "What fun would there be in that?"

"I would think very little."

He smiled and gestured at the sizable tapestry now overlooking the great hall. "So, what do you think, my lady?"

"Grace," she said softly. "If we are starting anew, I insist you call me Grace."

"Grace, then," he said just as softly, relishing the taste of her name on his tongue and her warmth on his arm once more. Her subtle, sweet scent. "What do you think of our tapestry's image?"

"I think it quite remarkable." Grace marveled at the view of the windswept sea and their castle from the woodland spot they visited when newly married. She swallowed hard, and her eyes grew glassy. "Utterly beautiful and very peaceful. A wonderful memory to revisit daily."

"Do you know why I had it commissioned?"

"Of course I do," she murmured, surprising him with how much her viewpoint aligned with his. "Because it was us looking at our lives from a distance, but no more." She shook her head. "Now the view is right here. We are part of it. Living it." Her gaze drifted to his face. "But more importantly, we are no longer running from it."

"I do hope we are not." He looked at the tapestry again when she did. "Though I imagine something so—" What was the word? How to say it correctly?—"*profound* would not happen overnight. So even though it seems we are here now, we are still making our way along but are closer now than ever?"

"Yes," she said, her voice soft again. "That is the perfect way to look at it."

While not saying she had forgiven him any more than her letter had, he felt like they were closer to peace. Closer to a new beginning born of truth. A place where their friendship, at the very least, might be resurrected and flourish.

"Show me what else changed in my absence, Charles." Her gaze roamed the hall, and she focused on several pieces they had purchased on a bright, sunny day, including a side table and a set of cushioned chairs they had bought, only to walk outside into torrential rain soon after. Used to getting wet and reflecting on his leaky carriage, they had dashed for the nearest pub. As if remembering how they had laughed, she smiled. "Show me everything on this floor, at least."

"Do you not wish to wait until tomorrow when it is brighter?"

Despite dining early, it was winter, and the sun had set earlier, so it was already dark.

"I see no reason to wait." Grace kept admiring the changes Charles had made. Hopefully, she remembered the moments attached to them as they'd shopped and got to know one another better. "You have clearly ensured all rooms are well-lit."

"I did," he admitted. "And while I allowed our servants to burn so many candles tonight so you might view what you missed while away, such will not be a regular occurrence. I hope to use less candlewax for the remainder of the winter. Not light anything at night save the rooms in use, whether to entertain guests for pleasure or business."

"It sounds like you are growing quite frugal."

"Do you disapprove?"

"Anything but." She kept taking things in and smiling on occasion. "I find myself rather hopeful. Quite optimistic if I were to be honest."

"Good." They walked from room to room, and he pointed out trinkets, furnishings, or tapestries they had purchased together, hoping she liked how he had presented them. "Everything can be moved around as you wish." Yet to keep on track as he took her past quite seriously and wanted her to understand he was not William. Would *never* be William. "I hired extra staff to clean the castle thoroughly for Alexander's sake, but many of them understand it is seasonal employment. Yet it's repetitive employment that will always be theirs if they do good work."

"And they were all right with that?"

"When told upfront, yes." He hoped she understood just how much his words pertained to their situation, too. That he said them not just because he intended to live by them but because he would only ever give her such as time went on. "It is when you tell someone a falsity when their wellbeing depends on truthfulness that people do not remain devoted. So, be it to strangers or to you, I will only ever be upfront going forward."

"I believe you mean that." Grace stopped and considered him most seriously, and searched his gaze for what seemed an eternity but was really only several long moments. "In fact, I rather think..." Her shoulders visibly relaxed, and she nodded, blessing him with trust he had feared lost to them. "No, not *think*, but know you do."

"I cannot tell you how glad I am to hear that."

She exhaled as though she had been holding her breath for years rather than seconds. "Nor am I that I feel such."

Her eyes lingered on his face momentarily as though she meant to say more but prompted them to continue strolling instead. "Thus far, I quite like where you have placed everything."

"I'm glad," he said. "There is still more to come. Items you may put wherever you like."

"Wherever *we* like," she corrected. "As I would much prefer refurbishing your castle together."

"*Our* castle," he reminded. "Very much our."

"Our," Grace said softly, pleased. She stopped at the doorway of the next room, and her eyebrows flew up. "I knew you had taken your ancestor down, but I had no idea you replaced him with another portrait." It displayed three boys astride horses. One wore breeches, and the other two, kilts. She smiled at the image to him as they drifted toward it. "Might I assume that is you, Blake, and Jacob when you were younger?"

"You might, because it is."

"How utterly perfect." Grace admired it and kept smiling. "A good display of how far things have come."

"Indeed."

"I am most impressed." A warm smile curled her mouth. "And I look forward to adding more portraits over the years. A means to share our life story, perhaps."

Did that mean they would resume being intimate? That they might share love in addition to friendship? While he wanted nothing more, he could admit to remaining fearful of losing another child. "I would like that."

"Yet you sound hesitant and appear troubled." She slowed again. "What is it, Charles? While you are clearly happy to have me and Alexander home, I cannot help but notice you seem a bit haunted, for lack of a better way to put it. There is a new sadness about you. Or perhaps worry. It is hard to pinpoint, but it is there."

He was not surprised she had caught such. That she already knew him as well as Thomas and Bessie. While tempted to keep it from her so she might enjoy her welcome home, he could tell by the concern in her eyes that he should not. Besides, he found he would prefer sharing. Allow her to understand him in a way so few did.

"If I were to be honest, it is what I spoke of before. A touch of melancholy left over from war." How best to describe it? "A mix of emotions ranging from fear and sadness to worry."

"I am so sorry to hear that." She looked at him with renewed concern. "What caused it? How can I help?"

"You are helping just by being here, Grace." He wanted her to understand how much she had changed things. "Just having you in my life has made a notable difference."

"Even when I was gone all these months?" she wondered. "While I had to take the time, please know I would have been here had the circumstances been different. As I said before, I want to be here for you always. Help you through if such is possible. Though I must confess, I fear not being good at it."

"You need not fear because you have already helped." He could not stop from touching her cheek and feeling her soft skin after what seemed like ages. "Although I missed you terribly, I have not suffered melancholy since you left. Instead, I have remained focused on improving myself and my surroundings. Being better so you and Alexander might have a good life here."

"Then why now?" As if she did not want to let the moment get too intimate, she continued strolling rather than leaning into his touch as she might have before. "What changed?"

"Nothing per se," he said. "If anything, my melancholy was triggered, for lack of a better word to explain it."

He proceeded to tell her why, including something he had not realized until now, only to wonder at the odd look in her eyes afterward.

Chapter Seventeen

GRACE HOPED CHARLES did not catch her response as to why he battled melancholy. How worrying over her and Alexander's safety when traveling had triggered something in him. A flashback of sorts. Apparently, fear over losing them had brought him back to those lost in battle and the loss of Charlotte and their unborn child.

That, in turn, had led to how fearful he would be if Grace ever became pregnant.

"So, you see," he said in conclusion, "you cannot be blamed because you knew no more than I that your trek home would invoke what it did. Yet, at the same time, it helped me better understand my deepest fears."

"Which is anything happening to me, Alexander, or our unborn child if I ever become pregnant," she said, trying to keep her tone gentle and supportive rather than crestfallen. The evening had been so lovely she had thought to tell him she was pregnant but now worried it might only add to his suffering. How would she ever tell him? Because she would have to soon.

"What is it, Grace?" He cupped her cheek again. "You seem…sad."

Sad? Perhaps. This was rather big news, and she wanted to share it with him. To have it bring him the same happiness it had brought her. But to realize he might see if differently…

"I am not sad but worried about you." Before, she had barely managed to pull free from his touch. This time, she was helpless against leaning into it. She had missed his warmth and feeling him so close. "Being the cause of your pain is the very last thing I want to do."

"You are not its cause, Grace. Ghosts of the past are," he said softly. Tenderly. "If anything, you are healing me."

"Yet you suffer still."

"Such does happen on occasion when one heals." His gaze lingered on her lips now. "What matters is I am improving. Just as you and Alexander have, yes? As our tapestry implies, we are pushing through the past to get to our future."

She tried to think clearly and respond but found it impossible when she became more aware of him by each moment. Lord knows she had been admiring him all night, but what rolled through her now was far more intense. An all-too-familiar ache that made her pull his lips down to hers before he could utter another word.

Kissing him again felt like coming home. Like being right where she was supposed to be. It also made her desire flare out of control. Clearly feeling the same, he groaned and cupped her backside. Squeezed her against him so she felt his arousal.

"If I keep kissing you," he murmured against her lips before he looked at her with unmistakable lust, "I fear I will not be able to stop."

She understood and felt the same. If they kept kissing, they would not make it upstairs. Nor did she want to. Not when she was so desperate. They were alone toward the back of the castle, so she glanced from a dark reading nook with nothing but a heavy velvet curtain for privacy and back to him. "Then do not stop, my lord."

Not needing to be told twice, he kissed her again, backed her into the nook, and shut the curtain behind them without his lips ever leaving hers. It was so dark she could hardly see him. She could feel the strength of his body, though. Smell his masculine scent. Hear his heavy breathing as he squeezed her lower half against him again and peppered kisses down her neck. She bit her lower lip hard when he caressed her pregnancy-sensitive breasts through her dress and suckled a pebbled nipple through the material.

"Charles," she gasped when he found his way beneath her dress and stroked the swollen flesh between her thighs, making sure she was ready for him.

When she squirmed against him and released a whimper of impatience, he seemed to understand because he backed her against the wall. Material rustled just enough to let her know he had freed himself.

Then he was there.

With her again, in a way she had missed so very much.

Her body pulsed with near-crippling anticipation as he lifted her skirts, hoisted her against the wall, and settled between her thighs. A fresh surge of excitement rushed through her at the position.

How he drew out the moment and let her lust build.

Rather than take her with one deep thrust, he allowed her to sink onto him so slowly, she whimpered again. This time with guttural pleasure at how good he felt. So good the moment he seated himself fully, her stomach quivered, ecstasy crashed over her, and release found her far too soon.

Seeming to relish the feeling of her pleasure, Charles groaned with approval and did little more than press deeper while she let go. In fact, he remained still inside her until her release simmered down to mild pulses.

After that, his strokes were long and intense.

Fast and heady.

Rather than cry out and be overheard, she wrapped her arms around him and buried her face in the crook of his neck. Heat built along with passion. Searing friction that made her groan despite herself and had tears rolling down her cheeks.

Made them breathe harshly as he drove them higher and

higher.

Nothing felt so exquisite than when she let go and soared over the edge again, giving into pure pleasure. She was so consumed by what he had wrung from her that it took several long minutes to realize he'd reached his pinnacle outside of her.

Even though she knew it was a testament to his fear of losing another child, it wounded her and felt personal even though it was not. She should talk to him and express her feelings. Tell him the truth that his seed had already begun to bloom inside her. Practice the honesty she wanted between them. But she felt too emotional for that right now and needed time alone.

So, she adjusted her clothing, pleaded exhaustion, and left their nook behind.

"Grace?" Charles caught her hand before she got too far, reeled her back into his arms, and cupped her cheek, looking at her with unmistakable concern. "What is it?"

She blinked back more blasted tears. "Nothing."

He frowned. "I thought we were done lying to each other?"

"We are." They should be, anyway. Yet she feared telling him the truth now and adding to the melancholy he fought. Not tonight. So, she thought quickly. "I suppose I just find myself overwhelmed with emotion." Not untrue. "Glad that Alexander and I are home and that you and I…" *Are having a baby together. A boy who might have your heroic spirit or a girl who might have your kind ways.* Of course, she said none of that and cleared her throat. "I am glad you and I are starting anew because I missed you."

"And I, you." He wiped away her tears and brushed his lips across hers. "So much that I hope you will sleep with me tonight and every night thereafter."

"And so I shall." But it could not be that night, when she felt so uneven. "Just not tonight, Charles. Surely, you understand how exhausting my journey?"

"Of course," he said. "Whatever you wish."

Yet she saw the disappointment in his eyes. Felt the same angst as he walked her to her bedroom, bid her goodnight, and kissed her one last time. Shortly after he went his own way, Catlin joined her to help prepare her for bed.

"Oh, dear," her maid said when she spied Grace's tears. "What is it? What happened, darling?"

"Truth told, only good things." She sighed. "Yet bad things to my way of thinking."

When Catlin looked at her in confusion, she explained Charles' fear over having a child together. "It seems he realized just how deep his concern was when he feared for me and Alexander's safety traveling here. If that were not enough, it gave way to a touch of post-war melancholy."

"I am so sorry to hear that." Catlin looked at her in understanding. "Now you fear telling him you are with child, I imagine? Fear you might only make matters worse?"

"I am." She clenched her hands together. "Because I will."

"Or—" Catlin gently closed her hands around Grace's to still them—"it might affect him the very opposite." She offered the motherly smile she had long perfected. "Whether Charles realizes it or not, it may be just what he needs to overcome his melancholy. Something that might put his demons to rest once and for all, or at the very least, help temper them."

"How so?" She frowned. "How when he fears such? When he seems so convinced the two are connected?"

"By seeing that you are not his late wife." She gave Grace a pointed look. "By being reminded how different you two are, then seeing it for himself as your pregnancy progresses. Seeing how strong and level-minded you are. By being convinced how much you want this child, so he need not fear losing either of you."

"All things he did not have with Charlotte," she murmured, thinking about it. "As she and I are very different." She frowned. "Even so, I have lost a child, which might very well perpetuate his fears."

"Then you need only remind him you carried a child to term shortly afterward." She pressed a gentle hand to Grace's abdomen in reassurance. "Then, if need be, make it clear you are already farther along than you were that first time. That *your* child, *his* child, possesses both of your strengths. That he or she is a fighter, indeed."

"Indeed," she said softly, resting her hand over Catlin's.

As always, her dear friend was right. While she would not talk to him tonight with her emotions running so high, she would soon. Tomorrow. That in mind and eager for the next day, she slept more peacefully than expected, only to find she had forgotten their plans when she arrived downstairs for breakfast.

Alexander, however, had not.

Chatting away about various things he hoped he might find as they explored the castle's hidden tunnels and rooms, her son brimmed with excitement. Meanwhile, Grace tried not to fret.

"It will be all right," Charles assured her when he spied her picking at her food. "I spoke with Alexander before you came downstairs. He understands that at the first sign of breathing difficulties, we will return to the regular part of the castle."

While tempted to inform Charles and remind Alexander it did not quite work that way, she did not want to take away from their excitement.

"In addition," Charles reminded, "as I said in one of our correspondences, me, Mr. Thomas, Mrs. Bessie, and a few well-trusted maids cleaned a great deal of it."

He *had* said that, and she appreciated it. She found it charming that Charles, an earl no less, had cared so much he had helped clean as well.

"I thank all of you for cleaning, Captain Charles," Alexander said dutifully. He cocked his head. "Though I do wonder if it was wise to share such locations with those outside our immediate family."

Charles chuckled and winked. "Rest assured, young Master, I made them sign a confidentiality agreement."

Alexander's eyes widened. "That sounds quite serious."

"It is," Charles confirmed. "So have no fear. Our castle's

secrets will remain most sacred."

She might be fretting, but she could not help but enjoy the two of them together. Alexander was happier than ever, and Charles? Remarkably good with children. So good, she knew he would be an outstanding father. More than that, if he saw one child come safely into this world, they might very well fill these walls with a sizeable family.

"Are we ready, then?" Charles asked after they finished breakfast. There was no missing his excitement when he stood and looked from Grace to Alexander. "For we have quite the adventure ahead."

Alexander stood and grinned. "I am ready indeed."

She stood and met their smiles. "Then I must be too."

Mr. Thomas had already brought in a satchel with coffee, a handkerchief for Alexander, and coats for all three as they would be traveling into colder parts of the castle.

"Excellent." Charles helped her and Alexander with their coats and inspected her son's handkerchief to ensure it was secured well.

"So, where do we begin?" Alexander asked when they were ready to go.

"Right here." Charles tossed him a mysterious smile and ran his hand alongside what appeared to be nothing more than built-in shelving. A click resounded moments later, and the shelving slid sideways to reveal a narrow doorway.

"I *knew* things were likely hidden in plain sight." Alexander's grin blossomed into a smile. "Yet I imagine there are things that are not." He notched his chin with determination. "Secrets even you have not discovered, Captain Charles."

"We shall see." Charles urged them to follow but to watch their step.

"Oh, my," she exclaimed as he lit a candle and led them into a stone corridor that seemed more out of the past than the castle itself. "This is something else, is it not?"

"It is," Alexander agreed, running his fingers along the cool, craggy stone.

"Just wait until you see what comes next." Charles urged them to follow him up a set of narrow winding stairs only to duck into a small room about a quarter of the way up, where his head nearly touched the ceiling. He pointed out the scant few arrow-slit windows. "While enemies lucky enough to infiltrate the castle and come upon this space might think this a room for archers, it was much more than that."

Alexander had a sharper eye than her because he narrowed in on a little bump under the throw rug. He pressed his foot over it and smiled at Charles. "This is an escape route, yes?"

"Quite right." Charles pulled back the rug, revealing a hatch door. "Centuries ago, this floor would have been covered with rushes instead of carpeting, making the handle impossible to see." He lifted the door to reveal a set of steep stairs. "The closer we near the sea below, the slicker the steps, so keep a firm hand on the railing."

Fortunately, they did not travel down too far before a flicker of daylight made seeing things easier. And what a sight as musty, damp rock turned to the scent of brine-ridden sea salt when they arrived in a cavernous area that overlooked the water.

"Look how close we are to the water now." Alexander stepped as close to the edge as she would allow him. "Perhaps one floor, if that."

"Indeed," Charles said. "Fortunately, this is high tide and as close as it gets, or I fear our castle would be more susceptible to structural damage during storms." He gestured at the entrance to a narrow tunnel that appeared to run alongside the sea. "That leads to several paths cutting up through the cliffs, offering both a perfect escape as well as a means for our warriors to position themselves in strategic locations if need be."

"How clever."

Charles and Grace exchanged a look that said Alexander need not know Longshanks likely had his say in its design if he had granted this land to Charles' ancestor. He was the sort of king who would have demanded all castles under his rule be built this way. She was surprised Hew had not shared such with Alexander yet, as she was sure he had researched it.

Instead of talking about tyrannical kings, Charles focused on other historical tidbits, such as the rusted wall brackets that had withstood the weathering of time. "Torches would be placed in those at night if attention needed to be called to a nearby ship."

"I see." Alexander inspected one of the brackets. "Should I assume they would light them for a ship to sail close for the family to flee or steer allies in for battle?"

"You should." Charles smiled with approval. "Very good, Master Alexander."

Clearly pleased with his praise, Alexander smiled in return and continued looking things over before Charles noticed her shiver from the wind coming off the sea and said it was time to resume the tour. There were still plenty of secrets to be had.

So, they made their way back up the steep stairs, through the latch door, then up the stairs they had first climbed to yet another narrow hallway. Charles explained how it ran the length of the first floor and showed them levers that would open hidden doorways to various rooms. He even opened them so they could see where they might end up.

"How remarkable," she said at one point. "There is a veritable castle within a castle."

"Very much so."

They started up a winding set of stairs that, amazingly enough, brought them into one of the lower watch towers.

"Several towers have them," Charles explained. "A means, of course, to sneak into defensive positions without infiltrators knowing."

"So those who took these routes would be making their final stance." Alexander seemed quite nostalgic as he peered out one of the arrow-slit windows. "If the enemy were already inside, their arrows would lessen their foe's numbers before they met their own end."

"Indeed." Charles shrugged. "If that is, this castle was ever conquered, which I am pleased to report it was not." He shook his head. "Proud English warriors all, my ancestors defended it well, and it never fell into enemy hands."

Alexander stood up a little straighter and nodded with approval. "I am equally pleased to hear that."

"I thought you might be." He gestured that they follow him. "Come, there is more to see yet."

It turned out there very much was. To the extent she only grew more shocked that so much could be hidden. Narrow hallways and several small rooms.

"It seems you and yours did a great deal of cleaning," she said to Charles, impressed as they made their way down a corridor toward one of three towers. It was impossible not to love him for all he had done. Thus far, she had not spied one cobweb nor any dust.

"And I appreciate it more than you know," she went on, stopping before they reached the tower Alexander had just rushed into. She brushed her fingers against Charles'. Hoped he understood just how grateful she was that he had cared to such an extent. Perhaps said too much without saying anything at all. "You will make a very good father, Charles. Already *are* a good father."

While she knew her words had a double meaning, he might not. Unfortunately, she had no chance to find out when a loud crash came from the room ahead, and a cloud of dust billowed down the hall.

If that were not daunting enough, her worst fear manifested moments later.

Chapter Eighteen

CHARLES HAD NEVER been so confused than when he made love to Grace the night before, only to have her shun him afterward. Because no matter how civil the end of their evening and her claim she needed rest might have been, it did not mirror the passion that had so quickly flared between them.

And what passion it had been.

He had never wanted to take a woman so much. Be between her thighs and deep inside her. Lose himself in all she could offer because it was so very much so with Grace. Almost too much if his heart were anything to go off. She filled it so entirely.

Filled it in a way that only fueled his desire for her.

There was no way to describe it other than to say Grace made him tirelessly hungry for her. Everything about her beguiled him from the moment she returned home to their every conversation since. So, when she finally pulled his lips to hers, a primal nature only she seemed capable of invoking had roared to the surface.

Granted, she and Charlotte were different women, but it had never occurred to him to act as impulsively with his former wife as he did with Grace. Then again, their passion had never been so intense, and their lovemaking so indescribable. Because there truly were no words to describe his near-frenzied need for her.

The raw, yet achingly loving way they came together.

So, he could not understand why she seemed so distant after their encounter when he'd never adored her more. He had thought he made her feel as good as she had him, yet things seemed strained afterward. Strained until this very moment in a hidden hallway as her fingers brushed his, and she told him what a good father he would make. *Did* make. Pulled him close again with a mere touch. Moreover, seemed to be trying to tell him something.

That is until they heard a crash ahead, and billowing dust filled the hallway.

Just like that, he was someplace else entirely, yet right there all at once. Standing in his castle's hallway yet on a ship filled with smoke. Trying to fight his foes. Save his countrymen gasping for air. For life.

And amid it all, Alexander gasped as well.

A truly vulnerable soldier who needed him more than anyone else.

So, rather than panic, his mind numbed as he straddled two realities and made his way through the cloying smoke. Fought blindness until he spied Alexander sitting against the wall. He had ripped away his face covering and gasped like a fish out of water.

Wide-eyed and pale, he struggled to pull air into his lungs.

Just like it had been on his ship that fateful day, terror struggled to break free, but Charles would not let it. Instead, everything inside him went perfectly, terrifyingly still, and he acted without thinking. He scooped up the wounded, determined to save him, and raced away from the smoke. Carried him free of the suffocating, unbreathable air.

Unlike the men he saved mid-battle, he would not leave this warrior. He was far too important. Yet he was not to be coddled either. That would do him no favors.

So he sat him against the wall and brought coffee to his mouth. "Drink, Alexander."

When the boy turned red and kept gasping for air, he cupped the side of his head and neck and made sure their gazes remained locked. Eased him from his terror as he would have his countrymen.

"You are free from harm now," he said sternly. "Feel that. *Know* it." He set the coffee down, rested his hand against the boy's chest, and willed him to live. Did not let him give in to his fear. "Focus on your inner calm and pull air into your lungs, son. Do you hear me?" He shook his head. "As your commander and captain, I give you no other option."

Alexander's eyes were wild with fear as his gaze remained on Charles' face, and he struggled to drag in air. Time sped up and slowed down all at once. Everything seemed suspended. His boy felt too far away. Without air for too long.

Leaving him.

Fading.

"Breathe, sailor, *soldier*," he said firmly, refusing to let him go. Not another under his watch. Not like this. Not this one. *Never* this one. "Breathe so that you might fight alongside me always. If not, I fear—"

Despite Alexander wheezing and his throat visibly striating as he struggled to pull in air, it seemed hearing what Charles feared made a difference because his boy finally, at last, pulled in air with such determination he knew he would be all right. Yet time was not to be wasted now any more than it would have been during wartime. Every measure must be taken. So he held the coffee to Alexander's mouth and urged him to drink after a few more deep breaths.

Once he was satisfied Alexander had begun to relax and his breathing evened, Charles plunked down beside him only for the boy to rest his head on his shoulder.

Had he gone too far?

Had he been cruel?

He had no idea. Not really.

Only then, as the numb place he had gone that fateful day years ago faded, and cold hard reality surfaced, did he realize concerned faces encircled them. Several servants, including Bessie and Thomas. Mrs. Catlin and Mr. Hew.

Most of all, though, Grace.

Beautiful, perfect, kind-hearted, his very dearest friend and love of his life, Grace. Her eyes were as wild with fear as Alexander's had been moments before, and her cheeks tear-stained as she dropped to her knees and cupped her son's face. She tried to speak, but nothing came out, so she tried again, finally finding her voice.

"How are you, darling?" she managed. "Are you breathing well now?"

"I am, Mother," Alexander managed weakly, clearly tired from the ordeal. "Thanks to Captain Charles."

"Without doubt, thanks to Captain Charles." She squeezed Charles' hand without looking away from Alexander. "I know it is early in the day, but why not go get some rest? This has been..."

When she trailed off, struggling against emotion, Mr. Hew crouched beside her and seemed to understand. "It has been a busy morning, Master Alexander." He pushed his spectacles up his nose quite firmly. "That said, perhaps you should take a brief respite before we begin our lessons for the day. Then, might we learn more about medieval English castles? Or maybe begin to create a map of the inner workings of this one, since the chances of enemy attack are probably lessened these days."

"Indeed, I would like that, Mr. Hew...but first..."

Charles bit back emotion when Alexander flung his arms around his neck and pressed his cheek against his chest. When he whispered so softly, he barely caught it, "Thank you, Father."

Then he was gone, joining Mr. Hew upstairs. But not before he heard Alexander make clear he would like to learn more about who had actually built this castle. How the monarchy might have influenced them at the time, and how that ruler might have also influenced other castles in England.

Charles could not help smiling at that. He appreciated that his boy was sharp. Paid attention. Not to mention highly observant, as Thomas explained after Alexander went upstairs. It seemed he had spied a notch in the hidden room's stonework nobody else had and, upon further investigation, slid a well-disguised exit aside only to discover a narrow circular tunnel going straight down.

A tunnel that exploded with ancient dust fueled by wind coming off the sea.

"We suspect it ends somewhere in the cave beneath the castle," Thomas said. "Given it has rusty footholds, it was likely an emergency route lest any kin ended up trapped at the top of the castle."

Charles nodded in acknowledgment but still felt much outside himself when Grace held out her hand to him and offered a soft smile he could stare at forever. A place so far beyond the terror of warfare and watching a child struggle to live, it seemed almost otherworldly.

"Come, darling," she said. "Let us take a few moments alone?"

"Of course, my love."

He followed her into his study, still feeling outside of himself. Not wholly aware of his surroundings. Still someplace else but at the same time, aware he was in his castle. Eventually, despite trying to avoid the dying flames on the hearth and slipping further into the violent memories fire could resurrect, he fell away. Lost himself. Yet he did not surface angry when he finally broke free.

Even so, time had been lost to him.

He knew it right away when he found himself sitting on the sofa but had no recollection of sitting down. Regardless, he felt at peace for the first time in longer than he could remember. Felt a sense of inner calm made all that much sweeter when he found Grace on the floor before him. As though she had been embracing him, her arms rested on either side of his legs on the sofa, and her cheek rested on his lap. Her breathing was so slow he knew she slept.

Determined not to disturb her, yet incapable of not touching her, he gently rested his hand on Grace's back only for her head to shoot up and her gaze to widen on him.

"Are you all right?" Enough worry flashed in her eyes to tell him she had seen another side of him. "Should I fetch Mr. Thomas or Mrs. Bessie?"

"No," he said gruffly, clearing his throat. He was overwhelmed to find her here like this when he had expected the opposite. "I have all I need right here…all I need in you."

"As do I here with you." She blinked back tears and cupped his cheek. "Do you have any idea what you did today? What a hero you are in every walk of life?"

He had never liked that label as it made one seem better than others when there were far more heroes walking the earth than anyone realized. "I do know what I did, and it was not nearly heroic." While tempted to shift away in shame, having her where she was, looking at him the way she did, was impossible to flee from. "I should have been more vigilant and discovered that trap door before Alexander did." He could not help but speak of the boy with pride. "Granted, he is bright and observant, but I should have been more so. I should have protected him."

"Yet you did." A tear slipped down Grace's cheek. "You protected him during the worst breathing episode of his life. Very much saved him and kept him with us, Charles. Loved him like he was your own son." Her voice softened. "And I was never so glad to see it because he *is* your son and you, his father now."

While he liked the thought of it, he wondered if she should too. Feared she might not understand. Even though he struggled to give her the truth, he did so because she deserved it. "I was having a war-related episode when I saved him, Grace." He shook his head. "I was not entirely myself, and that should terrify you."

"I agree." Grace sat on his lap, cupped his cheek again, and looked at him in a fashion that made the world fade away. "You were not entirely yourself but partly the man you once were. A warrior caught in battle. And I can tell you, without hesitation, you were as exceptional then as you are now." She shook her head and looked at him with her heart in her eyes. "Charles, even at your worst, you are the very best."

Before he could respond, she went on.

"So says this," she whispered, running her finger over his eyebrow and alongside his destroyed eye before she traced his scar. "And this. Both beautiful parts of you. Parts that tell your story. That tell—"

Horrified, he grabbed her wrist when he realized she had just run her fingers over an area beside his eye she should not have been able to touch. No doubt ripped off by him as he tended to do during his war-related states, his patch was gone. Laid bare for the first time outside of Thomas, Bessie, and the doctor who had taken his eye post-battle, he felt embarrassed and vulnerable.

"No." Grace shook her head and leaned into him when he thought to remove her from his lap and look for his patch. His safety net. "Wear it around others if you wish, but you do not need to with me, Charles." She steered his gaze back to her face when he thought to look away in shame. "I think you remarkably handsome without it."

"Then you are blind," he grunted. "And too kind by far."

"Too kind?" Grace shrugged. "Perhaps sometimes." She issued a small smile and teased. "As to being blind, I think that more your hindrance than mine in more ways than one."

Unsure how she did it when his flaws were so gruesome, he could not help but enjoy her pun. "Even so."

"There is no *even so*." She kissed him before he could shy away. Softly at first until she deepened it and fueled him into a passion of which only she was capable. A passion that kept him from fighting her when she hiked up her skirts and straddled him.

However self-conscious he might be, his arousal made it difficult to think when Grace continued kissing him and ground against him. She made it impossible to focus when she freed his arousal and sank onto him. When she showed him just how ready she was for him.

How aroused he made her despite his flawed face and

wounded soul.

"I think perhaps you do not understand how much I have come to love you, Charles," Grace said softly, cupping both his cheeks now. "How much you have proven time and time again how worthy you are of love in general. No matter your past, you have always been loving. And now you are much loved in return." She dropped soft kisses along his scar. "Whether it be the times your mind reverts to war." Another incredibly gentle kiss where his eye used to be. "Or those when you feel insecure." When her gaze found his face again, she was so compassionate and passionate at once, he knew she saw all of him. "Just as I was insecure before I met you."

Before he could respond, she kissed his mouth again and rolled her hips, making him feel such ecstasy with a mere movement that he could not help but groan. He reached beneath her skirts and clasped her backside. Held her in place and relished the feeling of her all around him. He wanted to touch her always. *Feel* her always.

"Insecure because of William's frivolousness," he managed, determined to keep with the conversation despite how she made him feel.

"Undoubtedly." She considered him. "But do you know what I realized through all of it? What you so recently helped me see?"

He looked at her in question and shook his head.

"That I am much stronger than I realized." Grace moved her hips again and kept him beneath her spell. "That no matter what happens, how hard marriage might be, I love with all my heart, and I do not waver." She rested his hand against her abdomen, and her eyes welled. "Might you do the same, my love? Might you, as you have shown time and time again, not waver? Because I am not just level-minded but a warrior. One who will never leave you." The corner of her mouth curled up. "And as you saw, my offspring tend to be warriors too."

Caught off guard, astounded, he could barely catch his breath as he looked from Grace's belly to her face. Dread mixed with elation. "You are…" He shook his head. "Should we be—"

"We should be, and I am." She brushed her lips across his, rolled her hips again, and kept her gaze locked with his. "And you will be as good a father to him or her as you are to Alexander."

"How can you be so sure?" he wondered, biting back a groan of pleasure before she closed her lips over his again, and all thought fled. Everything but Grace and how she made him feel. Not just that night, either, but well into the future.

Because, as it turned out, she was right.

Grace not only gave birth to a beautiful and very healthy baby girl five months later but several children as the years rolled on. So many that it was a good thing they had a sizeable castle.

Alexander grew into a fine young man who contributed to the architecture of many notable structures throughout Great Britain, Ireland, and Scotland. If that were not enough, thanks to Grace's unending support, Charles' emotional war wounds lessened with time, and he finally felt like he had made his ancestors proud.

Her proud.

So, in the end, despite his reservations, he was nowhere near being a second-hand earl, after all. If anything, to his wife's way of seeing things, he had been the best sort of earl England could hope for.

The sort of man their beloved country would only ever be proud of.

A credit he gave solely to Grace until their dying breaths because she and all the love she brought into his life had made all the difference. Love when he thought all hope was lost. Love that would give way to many generations who would, indeed, fill their castle walls with more memories than either could have ever dared hope for.

THE END

While saddened by the loss of her husband, Lady Abigail is determined to start life anew. Better still, she is determined to find freedom and adventure beyond her stuffy townhome and never, but *ever*, marry again. Or so she thinks until Maude and Blake are up to their old matchmaking tricks, and she finds herself pursued by an American businessman who will not take no for an answer in *Second Thoughts About the Heir*.

About the Author

Sky Purington is the bestselling author of over fifty novels and novellas. A New Englander born and bred who recently moved to Virginia, Purington married her hero, has an amazing son who inspires her daily and two ultra-lovable husky shepherd mixes. Passionate for variety, Sky's vivid imagination spans several romance genres, including historical, time travel, paranormal, and fantasy. Expect steamy stories teeming with protective alpha heroes and strong-minded heroines.

Purington loves to hear from readers and can be contacted at Sky@SkyPurington.com. Interested in keeping up with Sky's latest news and releases? Either visit Sky's website, www.SkyPurington.com, join her quarterly newsletter, or sign up for personalized text message alerts. Simply text 'skypurington' (no quotes, one word, all lowercase) to 74121 or visit Sky's Sign-up Page. Texts will ONLY be sent when there is a new book release. Readers can easily opt out at any time.

Love social networking? Find Sky on Facebook, Instagram, Twitter, and Goodreads.

Want a few more options? "Follow" Sky Purington on Amazon to receive New Release Kindle Updates and "Follow" Sky on BookBub to be notified of amazing upcoming deals.

www.ingramcontent.com/pod-product-compliance
Lightning Source LLC
Chambersburg PA
CBHW070353200726
48294CB00003B/889

* 9 7 8 1 9 6 0 1 8 4 3 4 4 *